Where Hedgehogs Dare

By Elizabeth Morley

Pour mon filleul, Antoine

Invasion. Everyone had known it was coming, and yet, when it did, they could hardly believe their eyes. Snippette was no different. She had spent all her life on Gruntsey, a tiny rural island where nothing much happened but life was pleasant and peaceful.

Then Hegemony had started a war. Invading one country after another, the Hegemons had gradually moved closer and closer to Gruntsey - repressing any opposition with a terrible brutality. Finally, they reached the Furzish coast. Only a narrow strip of sea separated them from Snippette's little island. Bristlin stood alone against Hegemony.

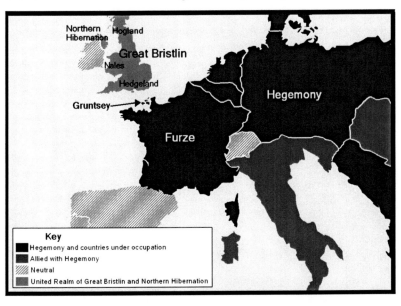

The Gruntsey Islanders, though mostly Furzish speakers and closer to the Furzish than the Bristlish coast, were nevertheless subjects of the Bristlish king. They depended upon the Bristlish Army for their defence and believed they would be protected; but the Bristlish Army was too weak and Gruntsey too close to occupied Furze. Instead, the Bristlish government sent a rescue ship so that any hedgehog who wished to leave could come to Bristlin. Snippette's brother Spike left and joined the Bristlish Air Force. Snippette stayed behind with her parents and watched as the Hegemons marched onto her beloved island and all contact with Bristlin was cut off.

It was not long before she regretted her decision to stay. Resistance was impossible on such a tiny island. There was nowhere to hide from the Hegemons, and any act of sabotage risked bringing a terrible retribution upon the whole population. It seemed that all she could do was sit the war out.

And that was what she did for a while. She stayed and carried on with her job in the local café; and, as they began to fear there would be food shortages, she helped her parents dig up their beautiful garden, pulling up the roses and lavender and planting vegetables in their place.

Sometimes, on her way back from the café, she sat on the esplanade and stared out to sea. Looking past the barbed wire and the guns, she focussed on the distant horizon as though, if she tried hard enough, she might catch a glimpse of Bristlin. She wondered how Spike was getting on there: she worried about him and at the same time she envied him - at least he was doing something.

"May I join you, *fraülein*?" asked a Hegemon officer one day as she was sitting on her bench. It was Major Dornig, the commandant for Gruntsey - Snippette had seen him before at the café. He smiled at her.

"You must do as you please," said Snippette icily.

"Zat is not a very friendly vay to speak," said Dornig, who nevertheless sat down.

"But you do, don't you?" retorted Snippette. "You *do* do as you please."

"No, I am a soldier: I obey orders."

"Hmph," said Snippette. She wanted to say more but dared not risk it. You could only go so far with these Hegemons before you found yourself locked up behind bars. So she got up and left the major to enjoy the view by himself.

As she walked home, she bristled with indignation and, by the time she reached her front door, she had made up her mind that, somehow, she would escape from Gruntsey. She would go to Bristlin, see her brother again and, above all, be free to do her bit for the war. Over the next couple of weeks, she formulated her escape plan. Then, once she had assured herself that it really could work, she paid a visit to her Uncle Stylus - her father's younger brother.

"Hallo, my dear," said her uncle with a smile, as he opened the door of his cottage to her.

"Hallo, Uncle Stylus," said Snippette, kissing him. "Are you alone? I need to speak to you."

"Well, yes, of course," said Uncle Stylus, though her cloak-and-dagger attitude worried him. "Come into the kitchen. I was just making a cup of tea. Do you want one?"

"Thanks." She sat down at the kitchen table and looked at him awkwardly for a moment. "Uncle Stylus," she said at last, "what made you decide to stay on Gruntsey once you knew the Hegemons were coming?"

"I don't know... I suppose I didn't believe they really would come. I think I expected we might at least get the chance to defend ourselves. I regret my decision now. I should have gone - I'm still young enough to fight - but what's done is done."

"But it isn't too late - you've got a boat," said Snippette. "You could escape."

"Escape!" he repeated, with a mirthless laugh. Then he looked at her earnestly with his kind eyes. "Don't get me wrong, Snippette. I've thought about it - but I try not to. There's no point dwelling on the impossible."

"I don't think it is impossible," she said.

"The place is a fortress, Snippette," he said firmly. "You know that."

"Every fortress has its weakness," retorted Snippette.

"My goodness! You really mean it, don't you? And I'll bet you've got it all worked out in that pretty little head of yours."

"That's right - I have," she said stoutly, needled by his tone.

"All right then," relented Stylus. "Let's hear it."

Putting her paw in her bag, Snippette brought out a map of Gruntsey, which she unfolded on the kitchen table.

"This map shows all the pre-war fortifications," she explained, "and I've marked the gun emplacements added by the Hegemons. All in all, as you suggested, they've got the coast pretty well covered. So one thing is clear: we *have* to go under cover of darkness."

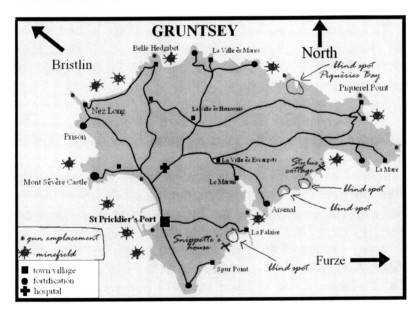

"Well, of course - if we could," said Stylus, "but, as you know, we're not allowed to take our boats out after dark. And the quay at St Pricklier's Port is well guarded - we can hardly slip past them unnoticed."

"So we take the boat out in daylight but make our escape by night," said Snippette.

"You're not making any sense. Look, if we didn't come back before dusk, they'd just come after us. - We'd get ourselves into pretty serious trouble, Snippette."

"I know - they've got enough look-out points to monitor your every movement if you're out at sea - north, south, east, west, it doesn't matter. But, look, if you stay close enough to the shore, there are several places where you can't be seen. I've marked the blind spots on the map. I reckon this one, Piquèries Bay, is the best. It's the most secluded, and the high cliff means the Hegemons have let up on the barbed wire and minefields. They probably also think there's no way up or down the cliff. Well, we know better. So, we leave your boat there and come back and collect it after dark on foot."

"But they'll still come after us. They've got a list of every hedgehog who's taken his boat out. If we don't come back, they'll know."

"But what's on that list? Just the name of the hedgehog and his passengers and the registration number of the boat. They don't note down the make of the boat or any kind of description, do they?"

"No," agreed Stylus.

"So we come back in a second boat - we come back in an inflatable dinghy with the same registration number painted on it."

Stylus looked at his niece in astonishment: "It's a very clever plan, my dear - I'll give you that, but I'm afraid it won't work. Some of the guards know me by now - and they know my boat. If I came back in an inflatable dinghy, they'd notice."

"I *was* worried about that," confessed Snippette, "but not any more. A couple of the guards were in the café the other day and I overheard one of them saying a new recruit would be joining them. His first shift is on Tuesday afternoon. So we go out on Tuesday morning and come back when the new guard is on duty; he won't have ever seen either you or your boat before."

Stylus really was amazed now - Snippette seemed to have thought of everything - but it was still incredibly risky. "All right," he said, "it sounds good in theory but any number of things could go wrong. And, if they catch us, there's no telling what they might do. I simply don't understand why you want to be taking such a risk. Me? I confess I'm very tempted. If I can get to Bristlin, I can join the Navy and help rid our country of these beastly Hegemons. But *you* can't fight, so what would be the purpose of you risking your life?"

"I want to do my bit," said Snippette firmly. "Even if it's just making widgets in a factory or working on the land. It all counts."

Snippette was nothing if not determined, and Stylus soon saw there was no point arguing. So it was that, two days later, the two hedgehogs went down to the quay at St Pricklier's Port, carrying fishing gear and a large bag containing an inflatable dinghy.

"Your papers," said the guard in his clipped Hegemon accent. Stylus showed him his fishing permit and their identity cards.

"*Gut, alles in ordnung,*" said the guard as he noted down the details. "You may pass."

They boarded the boat, and Snippette stashed the bag beneath the seats. Then she joined her uncle in the cabin.

"Well, Uncle Stylus, we've got three hours before the guards change. What do you say to a bit of fishing?"

Stylus smiled at his niece and took the boat out to sea...

Two and a half hours later, Snippette checked her watch: it was time to move. She took up the anchor and Stylus pulled in the fishing net. Then they set off towards Piquèries Bay, where they weighed anchor again - as close to the shore as it was safe to go. Snippette looked up at the cliff tops: it was just as she had hoped - they were completely hidden from the Hegemon look-outs. She pulled out the bag she had hidden under the seats and removed the inflatable dinghy and pump. Ten minutes later, the two hedgehogs had transferred to the dinghy and were on their way back to St Pricklier's Port.

As they approached the port, Stylus slowed the boat and scanned the quay. Snippette had been right. The guard had changed and the hedgehog who had taken over was a new face - just arrived in Gruntsey, Snippette had said. How she managed to glean these bits of information from waiting at tables in a café was beyond him.

"Ze fishing vas gut?" enquired the guard trying to be friendly, as they came alongside. "You haf many fish caught?"

"Yes - many," said Uncle Stylus, trying not to sound nervous as the guard checked their papers.

"Sank you," said the guard, returning the papers with a click of his heels and a nod. "*Guten abend*!"

Spike returned to his cottage but dropped Snippette off at her parents' house so she could spend her last few hours with them. At ten o'clock, she said her goodbyes, amid tears and hugs; then she slipped out into the night.

Walking along the quiet lane by the light of the moon, her footsteps seemed loud. She walked quickly, though she had plenty of time, and had covered near on a mile in fifteen minutes when suddenly the horizon ahead was lit up with the headlights of an oncoming car. Darting into a field, she dropped down into the grass. The car drew closer, slowing as it approached, and she could feel her heart thumping inside her. Then the car took a turning to the left and disappeared into the night. Breathing a sigh of relief, Snippette picked herself up and dusted herself off. Then she turned off into the fields: it would be safer, she decided, to complete the journey cross-country, where there was no chance of meeting anyone. The going was slower now and she occasionally stumbled as she walked over the uneven ground; but she had no fear of getting lost: she knew the island like the back of her paw.

At ten to eleven, she arrived on top of the cliff above Piquèries Bay. There was no sign of Stylus. Shining her torch along the cliff edge, she located the path which descended to the beach. Then slowly and carefully, she made her way down along its steep and twisting route until at last she felt the comforting scrunch of soft sand beneath her boot.

"Psst!" whispered a disembodied voice. "Over here!"

"Uncle Stylus?" whispered Snippette in her turn. "Is that you?"

The figure of a hedgehog appeared from nowhere, silhouetted against the night sky.

"Yes, it's me, my dear," said the figure.

The two hedgehogs hurried to the water's edge and out along a ledge of rock until they were within several feet of Stylus's fishing boat. They changed into their swimming costumes, threw their bags over into the boat and then swam across.

Snippette shivered as she towelled herself down in the cold night air; but soon they were dry and dressed and ready to go. She pulled up the anchor and Stylus started the engine.

"They won't hear us, will they?" asked Snippette suddenly, startled by the sound of the engine in the stillness of the night.

"Not if we keep the engine low," said Uncle Stylus; and, so saying, he guided the gently chugging boat out of the bay and into the open sea.

At first, the mildest of sea breezes merely ruffled the surface of the sea, and the going was good. But very gradually the wind grew stronger. Angry clouds gathered above them, blotting out the moonlight and the stars. Thunder rumbled in the distance, followed seconds later by a flash of lightning. Then the heavens opened. Rain pelted down and the swell of the sea tossed the little boat from wave to wave, showering her with its salty spray. Uncle Stylus peered through the rain-streaked window of his cabin and, gripping the wheel tightly in his paws, steered the boat head-on into the waves to prevent her from capsizing. Outside, buffeted about by the rain and the wind, Snippette scooped the water up from the bottom of the boat. Hour after hour, bucket after bucket, she carried on - through the night until at last the storm subsided and the danger was past. Exhausted and soaked through, she curled up on the seat and slept.

Several hours later, Snippette was startled from her sleep by the sound of gunfire. Hardly knowing whether she was dreaming or not, she dropped down onto the floor of the boat and peered over the edge. It was light now, and her heart skipped a beat, for the white cliffs of Hedgeland - the southern coast of Bristlin - were scarcely a quarter of a mile away. Uncle Stylus cut the engine and joined her, crouching in the bottom of the boat.

"Why are they firing at us?" asked Snippette, indignantly. "They can hardly mistake our little fishing boat for a Hegemon invasion force!"

"They probably think we're spies," said Stylus, "but I don't think they're trying to sink us or they'd have done it by now."

"Do you have anything white?" asked Snippette.

"Just my shirt," said Stylus, shivering as he took it off and attached it to a broomstick, which he clutched in his paws. He raised the broomstick above his head, and the two hedgehogs waited with bated breath as the bullets continued to fly. Then, as suddenly as the firing had started, it stopped. Very slowly, Snippette and Stylus stood up, their paws raised in surrender.

A boat came out to meet them. On board were five Bristlish hedgehogs in navy uniform - one at the wheel, the other four standing with guns trained on the fishing boat. As they came alongside, two of the sailors jumped across. Snippette and Stylus stood silent and nervous as they were pawcuffed and a thorough search was made of the cabin and the baggage under the seats. Finally, they were towed ashore, put in the back of an army truck and driven to an anonymous suburban house.

Stylus was led into a back room and Snippette into a room upstairs. As she entered, a hedgehog in army uniform stood up and indicated that she should take the chair opposite him. She sat, and the hedgehog who had escorted her uncuffed her and left. Snippette waited for the army officer to speak but he said nothing. She tried to make out his face but was blinded by the lamp on the table between them which shone directly in her eyes. Looking away, blinking, she noticed that the black-out blind was pulled down though it was broad daylight outside.

"*Wie heissen Sie?*" - the officer spoke at last.

"I'm sorry?" responded Snippette, who had hardly expected to be addressed in the Hegemon language - she supposed it must be a trap in case she were a Hegemon spy.

"What's your name?" repeated the officer, reverting to his native Hedgelandish; there was an icy edge to his voice.

"Snippette," she answered nervously.

"Where have you come from?"

"Gruntsey."

"Why did the Hegemons allow you to leave?"

"They didn't. We escaped."

"Who helped you?"

"No one."

"Who else knew about the escape?"

"Only my parents."

"Gruntsey's a virtual fortress," declared her interrogator. "It's impossible to leave unnoticed."

"Every fortress has its weak points," began Snippette; and gradually she forgot her tiredness and the stress of her situation, as the excitement of her adventure was rekindled within her. "If you stick close to the shore," she continued, "there are several blind spots - places to hide a boat..."

Snippette related the story of their escape down to the last detail. Her interrogator listened impassively, silently making notes.

"Is there anyone in Bristlin who can vouch for you?" he asked, when she had finished.

"Yes, Spike, my brother - he's in the Air Force."

"All right. You can rest now."

He left the room, locking the door behind him, and Snippette went and curled up on the bed. But she could not sleep - tired, excited, fearful, her mind tossed this way and that. She had never imagined that she would be locked up as a suspected Hegemon spy on arrival in Bristlin. She had expected to be welcomed - congratulated, even. What if she could never convince them of her innocence? What would happen to her then? She wiped away a single tear, which had escaped from her half-shut eyes, and tried to think more positively. Then the door opened and a new army officer came in the room. Snippette raised herself wearily from the bed - she had been allowed to rest for barely ten minutes.

"How do you do, Miss Snippette?" said the newcomer in a friendly tone. He offered his paw, which she shook hesitantly. "I'm Major Hedges. Please, won't you sit down?"

Snippette sat down, wondering whether she was being subjected to the 'hard cop-soft cop' routine she had seen played out at the cinema.

"Major Beastie tells me you have a very interesting story to tell. I'd like to hear it from you."

* * *

Snippette soon lost all track of time. The incessant questioning, the interrupted sleep, the constant repetition of the same story gradually wore her down until she sorely regretted her decision to come to Bristlin. She had been a fool to think she could just turn up and be accepted for who she was in the middle of a war. She thought of Uncle Stylus downstairs - Uncle Stylus who would have been safe at home had it not been for her, and her conscience pricked her.

On the fifth or sixth session, as she sat there explaining her story to Major Hedges for the umpteenth time and wondering how much more she could take, her attention was momentarily distracted by the sound of a car drawing up in the drive just below her window.

"Ah, yes," said Major Hedges, "there's someone I'd like you to meet. Why don't you take a look?"

Snippette went over to the window, lifted the black-out blind and peered down. Two hedgehogs got out of the car. The driver she recognized as Major Beastie; the passenger was an Air Force officer. She rubbed her eyes and stared...it could not be...but yes it was! Snippette gave a little shriek of delight and spun round to face the major.

"It's Spike, my brother!" she exclaimed.

"Good, you've passed the first part of the test," said the major, smiling.

"I'm sorry?" responded Snippette, puzzled.

"You've identified Flight Lieutenant Spike correctly," explained the major. "Now, for the final part of the test - if you could just bear with me a little longer - I'd like you to sit quietly, please, and, when the lieutenant comes in the room, say nothing."

Snippette did as she was told. A minute later, there was a knock on the door and Spike walked in. Snippette looked at him expectantly, her eyes bright with excitement, but said nothing.

"Snippette!" exclaimed Spike, who had clearly not been told whom he was to meet. "I can't believe it! How on earth...?"

Snippette could contain herself no longer. She leapt up from her seat and threw herself into her brother's arms.

"Ahem." It was Major Hedges. Snippette drew away from her brother. "I'm sorry to break up the family reunion," said the major, "but, Flight Lieutenant Spike, I'd be grateful if you'd formally identify this hedgehog and her relationship to you."

Spike did as he was asked and, at last, Major Hedges seemed to be satisfied. He even left the room so that they could have some time alone together, and a few minutes later Uncle Stylus joined them. Stylus was smiling for, like Snippette, he was a free hedgehog again. Then Major Beastie reappeared.

"Well, I expect you'll all be wanting to make a move shortly," said Beastie. "Before you do, though, I should like to have a word with you alone, Snippette."

Little shivers ran down Snippette's spines. "Yes, of course," she said faintly, and the others left the room.

"Please, take a seat," said Beastie. Snippette sat. "You said, during the interrogation, that you wanted to do your bit for the war. Do you have any particular thing in mind?"

"No, not really - I'll do anything, so long as it helps."

"Even if it's dangerous?"

"Yes, even if it's dangerous," said Snippette, wide-eyed.

Beastie smiled - it was the first time Snippette had seen him do so. "I can well believe it after that escapade of yours," he said. "And you're bilingual, you said? You speak both Hedgelandish and Furzish?"

"Yes, for most Gruntsey islanders Furzish is their first language," said Snippette. "But I grew up speaking Furzish with my mother and Hedgelandish with my father - his family originally came from Bristlin. And I lived in Furze for a while, too, when I was studying cookery."

"Good - very good. Now tell me," added Beastie, leaning forward, "how would you feel about doing secret work? Work which you wouldn't be able to tell anybody about? - Not even your brother or uncle."

"Well, if it were necessary, then I'd accept that."

"It is," said Beastie emphatically. "Let me explain: I have a colleague in a secret organization known as F.L.E.A. - the Field Liaison and Espionage Agency. F.L.E.A. trains hedgehogs in sabotage, espionage and other clandestine activities, and then parachutes them behind enemy lines, where they can hit the enemy hard. It's dangerous work. If you're caught, you'll almost certainly be shot...and, before they shoot you, they will probably torture you to extract as much information as possible."

Snippette stared at Beastie in astonishment, half appalled, half excited.

"F.L.E.A. are always on the look-out for recruits," continued Beastie. "They're looking for hedgehogs who are bilingual, courageous, clever and discreet. I think you fit the bill. What do you think?"

* * *

That evening, Spike found Snippette and Stylus lodgings in north Lairden, near his Air Force station. He had two days' leave, so the three hedgehogs decided to have a bit of fun together - seeing the sights, window shopping, dancing the night away. However, at the end of his leave, Spike went back to work, flying reconnaissance missions over enemy territory; and Stylus went to the War Office to volunteer for the Navy. Snippette was alone.

She did not move at first but sat on her bed, staring at a piece of paper on which Major Beastie had scrawled an address. Eventually, however, she roused herself, drew a deep breath and went out into the street.

"Taxi!" she called, raising her paw.

"Where to, miss?" asked the taxi driver.

"103 Sharpesbury Avenue."

Number 103 Sharpesbury Avenue was an anonymous-looking stone building with double doors up a short flight of steps. Snippette rang the bell and was let into a large entrance hall, in the middle of which sat a hedgehog in army uniform.

"Good morning. I have an appointment with Brigadier Scrape. My name's Snippette."

"Um...yes, of course. Please go up. You'll find the brigadier in room 5 - first floor, third door on the left."

Snippette made her way upstairs and knocked on the door of room 5.

"Enter!" said a clipped, military voice.

Snippette entered. Brigadier Scrape sat with his feet up on a large oak desk, wearing an enigmatic smile on his face and a patch over one eye.

"Good morning, sir. I'm Snippette."

"How d'you do, Miss Snippette," said the brigadier, standing up and shaking her by the paw. "Please, take a seat."

She sat.

"Major Beastie speaks very highly of you. But, of course, I shall have to make up my own mind."

"Of course, sir", said Snippette. A silence followed, which Snippette assumed was intended to unnerve her. She recognized the technique from her interrogation by Major Beastie.

"Are you afraid to die?" asked the brigadier suddenly.

Snippette thought for a moment. "Yes, sir."

"Then what the blazes makes you think you could work for an organization like F.L.E.A.?" barked the brigadier.

"Some things are more important to me than my fear of dying," explained Snippette.

"That's all very well, but it isn't enough to act in spite of your fear - you have to conquer it. A nervous agent is a dead agent - and, what's more, he's a danger to others."

"Of course," said Snippette. "I really just meant that I prefer to stay alive. If I had a mission to focus on - to think about, I believe I could overcome my fear."

"I understand that your escape from Gruntsey was entirely of your own devising?"

"Yes, though I could never have done it without my uncle. He's a much better sailor than I am."

"You're anxious to share the honours."

"Just factual."

"Major Beastie said you'd lived in Furze as a student. *Vous avez des amis là-bas?*"

"*Oui, la famille avec laquelle j'ai vécu. Mais je n'ai plus de ses nouvelles depuis le début de la guerre.*"

"Your Furzish is very good."

"I'm bilingual."

"You're very confident of your ability. Do you really consider your Furzish to be flawless?"

"Yes. It isn't a boast - I'm just being factual, sir. I grew up speaking both languages."

The brigadier smiled. "Well, Miss Snippette, I think I can endorse Major Beastie's assessment. Welcome to F.L.E.A.."

* * *

On Sunday morning, Snippette packed her bags and, following the brigadier's instructions, took the 2.50 train from Paddalong Station. On the way, she posted a letter to Spike telling him she had joined the Land Army and gone to work on a farm; she left a similar note for her uncle.

The train took Snippette deep into the countryside of southern Hedgeland to a sleepy little village called Gorsley. No-one else got out at this station but a car was waiting for her outside, with a jolly driver who smiled a lot and introduced herself as Corporal Bramble. The corporal took Snippette along a maze of narrow country lanes for about a mile and then turned in at a pair of wrought iron gates flanked by armed sentries and barbed wire. "Hallo, Private Pike," said the corporal, with a cheeky smile and a wave of her identity card; then she swept through the gates and up the gravel driveway, finally coming to a halt in front of a large stately house.

"This is us, ma'am," said Bramble as she applied the brake. "Gorsley Manor - home of F.L.E.A.. If you go inside, you'll find the other trainees having tea in the drawing room. I'll take your bags to your room."

Snippette found the drawing room lively with the chatter of ten or fifteen hedgehogs. She noticed that most but not all were in uniform.

"Hallo there," said one, "I don't think we've met. I'm Sub-Lieutenant Clipper and this is Nurse Teasel."

Snippette introduced herself and shook the proffered paws.

"Have you seen your timetable yet?" asked Teasel.

"No, I've only just arrived," said Snippette.

"Not to worry," said Teasel. "I'll show you the notice board. Clipper, be a dear and fetch Snippette a cup of tea, will you?"

They scanned the notice board for Snippette's name. Her first session was an introduction to the make-up of the Hegemon army, at 9:00 hours on Monday morning. This was to be followed by classes in telegraphy, cryptography, secret writing, the Hegemon language and parachuting.

* * *

The training was hard but Snippette enjoyed the challenge. Every morning began with a run around the park and over an obstacle course, and finished with fifty press-ups. In the second week, she moved on to escape and survival techniques and paw-to-paw combat. Then she was taken to a firing range, taught to fire a variety of weapons and introduced to explosives. However, half way through this, she was suddenly summoned by Brigadier Scrape.

"I'm afraid I'm going to have to pull you off the course, Snippette," said the brigadier.

"Pull me off the course?" repeated a shocked Snippette. "Wasn't I up to scratch, sir?"

"So you won't be doing any demolition or bomb disposal," continued the brigadier, who appeared not to have heard, "but I doubt there'll be much call for either of those."

"Sir?" said Snippette, who was visibly upset, if only the brigadier had been looking.

"And the fact is that we have no choice," said the brigadier, gazing out of the window. "We've just received secret intelligence that Hegemony has set the date for the planned invasion of Bristlin - September the 15th. Beyond that we have no information at all. They'll launch the invasion from Furze, of course. And it's likely that they'll attack somewhere along the southern coast of Hedgeland, but it's a big area to defend and, in any case, we could be wrong. We also know nothing about the make-up, size or disposition of the attacking force. Your mission, should you choose to accept it, is to find these things out."

Snippette gaped at Brigadier Scrape. The shock of disappointment had gone, only to be replaced by the shock of being entrusted with such an important and yet seemingly impossible task. "Me, sir? Why have you chosen me?"

"The Château Grif, where the invasion plans are being kept, is in the region of Prickardy in northern Furze. You know the area well, you're bilingual and you've shown a great aptitude for this kind of work. We also think the operation may benefit from, let us say, the feminine touch."

"How am I to get into the château?"

"That, I'm afraid, is something you're going to have to work out for yourself, once you get there. We've very little information about the place. However, there is someone who may be able to help you: a Furzish hedgehog by the name of Clou. He's the Comte de Grif and the Château Grif used to be his home before the Hegemons made it their army's H.Q. in northern Furze. Clou knows the château like the back of his paw."

"Clou will help me get into the château?" queried Snippette.

"In and out - the second bit is just as important," said the brigadier. "At least that's what we hope he'll do. Clou has disappeared off our radar, so to speak. We think he's in the Clawdogne region in southern Furze, where he has a cousin - Clousette. I'm afraid we haven't been able to contact either of them. So you're going to have to make a detour to the Clawdogne to find him."

"Won't this all take too long, sir? If time is so short?""Time will be tight, certainly, but we can't afford to cut corners. We just don't have adequate information about the château. If you can't get into the château or you're caught, the mission will have failed - and there's too much depending on it. Before you go, if the weather clears up, we should have some air reconnaissance photographs for you and that'll give you an idea of the kind of security they've currently got on the outside. But only Clou can give you a plan of the interior."

Snippette was given three days to prepare for her mission. She was told to keep her real name, which was common enough in Furzish, but was given a fake life history to memorize and a forged identity card to go with it. No time was wasted: she was expected to start learning her cover story straightaway and warned that she would be grilled on it that afternoon. Word-perfect would not be enough: she needed to be able to recite her story naturally - like something she had lived through and not simply learnt by wrote.

When she broke for lunch, she rang Spike. She wanted to speak to him before she left, as a kind of goodbye, even though she could not say where she was going.

"Are you all right?" asked Spike. "Only you sound sort of funny."

"No, I'm fine. What about you? Are you all right?"

"Right as rain," said Spike cheerily. "I've been grounded for the last few days because of the weather but it's clearing up now. Anyway, old bean, were you ringing up about anything in particular or just because you love the sound of my voice? - Only I've got to go in a second."

"Nothing in particular," said Snippette. "Just look after yourself."

"I will," said Spike. "Lots of love..."

Spike frowned as he put the phone down. Snippette had certainly sounded odd - maybe she was missing home. He decided to take her out to dinner once he got back from his mission. Then he pushed her out of his mind and focussed on his job. It was a slightly unusual one this time - the Château Grif in Prickardy. Normally they photographed military and naval dispositions, factories, railways - that sort of thing. But, as far as he knew, this was just an army H.Q. with a few senior officers sitting behind desks. Still, it had to be pretty important - he had been allotted a flight from a fighter squadron to escort him as far as the Furzish coast, and that was a first. Well, ours not to reason why, he thought to himself, as he clipped himself into his emergency parachute and walked out onto the airfield.

His fighter escort was already out there, all set to go. Squadron Leader Hotspur, who was seated in the cockpit of his aeroplane, tapped a claw impatiently against the fuselage. "Come on Spike, old chap, we haven't got all day."

"Sorry, sir - telephone!" explained Spike. He jumped up into his own plane, turned on the engine and watched the propellers spin into action and then disappear into a blur. Taking the aeroplane forward, he bumped along across the uneven tarmac, going faster and faster, until he was speeding towards the end of the runway...then the plane lifted and he was off.

The four aeroplanes soared up into a clear blue sky, and Spike smiled to himself as he felt the tingle of excitement in his spines: he loved flying - war or no war, it was sheer exhilaration to him. He looked down admiringly at the patchwork of hedges and fields, farm tracks and gently meandering streams. Then he pulled down his goggles and focussed his mind on the horizon and Furze.

They had a clear run all the way down to the sea. Soon they were halfway across and within ten miles of the Furzish coast.

Far below an enemy ship opened fire but they were well out of range. A futile gesture, reflected Spike. Then the crackle of his radio interrupted his reflections.

"Hallo, Hedge Hopper. Hallo, Hedge Hopper. Road Hog here. Do you read me? Over." It was Squadron Leader Hotspur.

Spike pressed the button on his mic. "Hallo, Road Hog. This is Hedge Hopper - reading you loud and clear. Over."

"Hedgehogs at five o'clock below," warned Hotspur. "You'd better get out of here. We'll keep them occupied."

"Willco, sir," said Spike, pulling his aeroplane up towards the sun, while his friends closed in on the four enemy planes below. Suddenly the sky was dotted with red flashes. A moment later a plume of smoke poured out from an enemy aeroplane as it nosedived; just beyond it a small figure drifted earthwards beneath a parachute.

All four enemy planes were fully engaged now, and Spike could leave without fear of pursuit. With a sudden burst of speed, he slipped over the hogfight towards the Furzish coast. He wanted to fight with them but could not: he had cameras under each wing and another one under the fuselage but no guns - he was fast but utterly defenceless. In any case, it was his duty to stay *out* of trouble and make sure he made it back to base with the photographs he had been told to take. That, after all, was the whole point of this little outing.

Spike sped on towards his target as fast as he could now. From here on he was unprotected, and it was highly likely that one or more of the enemy aeroplanes would survive the encounter with his friends and give warning of his approach. The more distance he could put between himself and the scene of the battle, the less likely it was that any reinforcements would find him. His goal was to get in quick, take the photographs and get out again even quicker.

Spike gripped the stick tightly in his paws as he flew in over the flat, open countryside of Prickardy, looking for any signs of the enemy but also for his target. So far all he had seen was the little brick villages so typical of the region, scattered about like tiny islands in a sea of wheat, and a network of ramrod straight roads and canals connecting them. But now there was a large and distinctive river over to starboard and beyond it a large brick building with a slate roof: the Château Grif at last!

Spike swept in low over the château and released the camera shutter - once, twice, three times. An anti-aircraft gun fired at him. As he swooped up and away, a spray of bullets clipped the edge of his portside wing, but the damage was not serious. He went in again and then a third time until he was satisfied he had at least a couple of good photographs in the bag.

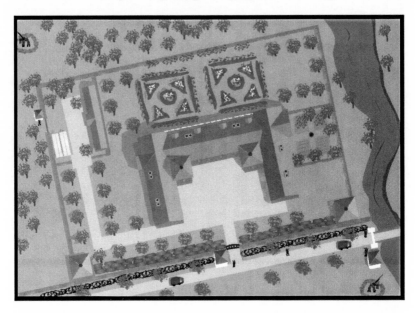

It was time to go home. Spike turned his plane westwards towards the Furzish coast, where the sun was sinking behind a thin bank of clouds; when it reappeared, he blinked in its glare. Then he blinked again as a cluster of black dots emerged out of the blinding light. The dots grew bigger - they were enemy fighter planes and they were coming straight for him.

Spike swerved away from the oncoming aeroplanes but then others appeared, as if from nowhere. Suddenly they were on his tail. Spike steep turned just as they opened fire. They overshot him but his plane had been hit - and badly this time: it was on fire and losing height - heading straight for the village below. Spike would not bale out for fear that the plane would crash into the village. Gripping the stick in his paws, he pulled the plane round towards a large grassy field as the ground rushed towards him. Then there was a thud and he was down, bumping along the field at high speed until his starboard wing smashed against a tree and he came to a halt on the bank of a canal.

Spike jumped down from the burning plane and hurriedly removed the film from the cameras, as a truckload full of Hegemon soldiers raced down the road towards the crash site. He did not hear them above the noise of the river and crackle of flames but there was a chance the aeroplane would explode, so he worked fast. As soon as he had removed all the films, he ran away from the burning wreck - then paused to look for cover. He swivelled round to survey the landscape but then stopped in his tracks: he was surrounded.

"*Pfoten hoch,*" said the hedgehog nearest him.

"What's that you say?" asked Spike, raising his voice a little to make himself understood. "*Sprechen Sie Hedgelandisch?*"

"Paws up!" translated the enemy hedgehog. "For you ze var is over."

* * *

Pacing up and down at an airfield on the south coast, Snippette looked at her watch: it was nine o'clock and her aeroplane was waiting for her. She was ready to go - she had already put on her flying overalls and a parachute but Brigadier Scrape, who was meant to be bringing the reconnaissance photographs of the Château Grif, was late. So she sat down, opened her case and checked the contents for the umpteenth time: clothes tailored in the Furzish style and with Furzish labels, a field radio, a bundle of Furzish money, maps, a skeleton key, wire-cutters, a forged identity card, a couple of food coupons, a letter in Furzish to support her cover story and a used railway ticket. It was all still there and all references to her real identity had been removed. Once she had found a safe place to hide the obviously dodgy items - the radio and maps etc., there would be nothing to incriminate her - nothing to suggest that she had ever been to Gruntsey or Bristlin. She closed the case and began to drum on it impatiently with her claws.

"Ah, good evening, Snippette." It was the brigadier, arrived at last. "I'm sorry I'm late - there's been a last minute hitch. I'm afraid you're going to have to do without the aerial photographs of the château. The pilot didn't come back. We assume he was shot down."

"Oh," said Snippette faintly. A sick, guilty feeling gripped her. With a brother in the Air Force, she had little difficulty imagining what the pilot's family must be going through.

"Well, the best of Bristlish," said the brigadier, as he gave her his paw. "There's a lot riding on your mission but, if anyone can pull it off, you can."

"Thank you, sir," said Snippette, pulling herself together; then she turned tail and walked out into the darkness towards the waiting plane.

The flight over to Furze was cold, noisy and uncomfortable. There were no windows in the back of the plane and only a hard bench to sit on. The co-pilot occasionally looked in on Snippette but, for the most part, she sat on her own - in the dark and alone with her thoughts. Until now she had been too busy to think much about the likelihood of success. Now she did have time to think and she knew there was a fair chance she would not get out of this alive; the chances of getting hold of the invasion plans and smuggling them safely back to Bristlin were even slimmer.

When the plane came over the Clawdogne region and it was time to jump, she was more relieved than afraid: action was preferable to thinking. She hooked herself up while the co-pilot opened the hatch. Then she sat down on the edge of the opening and stared out into nothingness. "Go!" said the co-pilot. She took a deep breath and jumped.

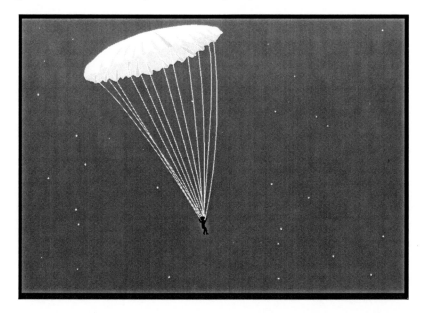

For a few long seconds, she was diving bullet-like through the void, cold air roaring in her ears, pummelling her body and pushing up the fur on her face. Then the parachute opened: her speed suddenly slowed and she drifted peacefully earthwards.

Looking down to where the dark sky merged into the blackness of the hills far below, she noticed directly beneath her two pinpricks of light. As they got closer, she saw that they were hedgehogs holding torches - members of the Furzish Resistance, who had been sent to meet her.

All of a sudden, the ground rose towards Snippette and she landed with a jolt. She rolled into a ball to break her fall, then picked herself up, unclipped her parachute and started gathering it in.

"I'll take that for you," said a voice in Furzish. "Snippette, isn't it? I'm Hérisse, and this is Grattain."

Snippette blinked and shook paws with the two shadowy figures: "Thank you for meeting me."

"No problem," said Hérisse. "Do you have your case? Good. Then follow me." Snippette followed the two Furzish hedgehogs to the edge of the field and through a wood. Walking in silence, they continued for about fifteen minutes until they reached a narrow lane. Three bicycles were waiting for them, propped against a tree. They took the bikes and rode to a secluded farmhouse, where they dismounted and went inside.

Hérisse led the way into a cosy living room and introduced his wife, Epine, who showed Snippette to her room. As soon as she was alone, Snippette locked the door behind her, took the radio out of her case and signalled F.L.E.A. H.Q..

"Broad Thorn calling Spiny Buoy. Broad Thorn calling Spiny Buoy. Come in Spiny Buoy. Do you read me? Over."

The radio spluttered and whined; then a faint voice responded.

"Spiny Buoy here. Reading you loud and clear. What is your message? Over."

Snippette pressed the button on her microphone.

"The hedgehog has landed...."

***

As she sat over breakfast with Hérisse and Epine the next day, Snippette got straight to the point.

"What have you been told about my mission?" she asked.

"Nothing at all," said Hérisse, shrugging his shoulders. "Just to give you every possible assistance. You must tell us what you want."

"I need to find a hedgehog by the name of Clou," said Snippette. "We think he's somewhere in the Clawdogne region but we've nothing more precise than that. I can tell you that he's the Comte de Grif and has a cousin in the area - her name's Clousette - but that's all. Do you know of him - or her?"

"No, I'm afraid not," said Hérisse. "We'll have a sniff around for you."

"Thank you," said Snippette; then she added hesitantly: "I don't like to push you but I've very little time...you will start looking immediately, won't you?"

"Naturally. I'll put every hedgehog I've got onto it."

Hérisse and Epine went out, leaving Snippette alone at the farm, and only reappeared in the evening. Snippette questioned them expectantly but they had had no luck - no one had heard of either Clou or Clousette. The next day they went out again but still made no progress.

"I can't wait indefinitely," said Snippette pacing up and down.

"We're doing our best," said Epine, needled by Snippette's obvious impatience. "The Clawdogne's a big region."

"Yes, of course," said Snippette, still pacing, "but time *is* very short. Perhaps I should come out with you tomorrow..."

"Come out with us!" exclaimed Hérisse in horror. "What would be the purpose? You don't have any contacts here and you'd only be drawing attention to yourself. You could get us all shot."

"No, sorry, you're quite right. But there must be *something* I can do. Perhaps I could get a job in town - keep my ears pricked."

"I don't know," said Hérisse doubtfully. "It's a very long shot. I'm not sure it's worth the risk."

"What isn't worth the risk?" asked Grattain, who had just let himself in.

Hérisse explained.

"No, I should say not," agreed Grattain. "I've just come from town and there's nothing - not a whisper. Nobody's heard of your hedgehog."

"Is that today's newspaper you've got there?" asked Snippette, ignoring Grattain's discouraging words. "May I have a look?"

Grattain gave her the newspaper. She opened it hastily at the back page and pawed over the job notices. "That's it!" she said triumphantly. "There's a vacancy at the Post Office! They'll have every hedgehog's address in the district."

The following morning, Snippette went into town with Grattain. The streets were busy with hedgehogs buying their morning bread or on their way to work. They were Furzish for the most part, but still you could never get entirely away from the Hegemons - officers driving through town in open-topped cars, soldiers patrolling the streets... It was all rather unsettling, though Snippette felt that she ought to be used to it by now; she had, after all, lived under occupation in Gruntsey. But then she had had nothing to hide; now she was living under a false identity and engaged in a hostile mission for which she could be shot.

She pushed the thought away. She had promised to focus on her mission - to exclude fear from her mind - and she would. Shaking paws with Grattain, she thanked him for his help and crossed the street to the Post Office. Happily, the glowing references which Epine had just forged for her did the trick. She got the job straightaway and was set to work, sorting the morning letters. Of course, the chances of coming across a letter to Clou or Clousette were extremely remote; but an index of every hedgehog's address in the region was kept locked up in the cupboard. Though Snippette's job sorting gave her no excuse for looking in the index, this was hardly a bar for a highly-trained F.L.E.A. agent.

The morning she spent chatting with the other employees, getting to know the layout and the routine. During the lunch break, she went outside and did a swift external recce before returning to work.

"Coffee break," announced the supervisor half way through the afternoon. The sorters stopped sorting and started to troop out of the door. Snippette dropped a letter on the floor and slowly bent down to pick it up, letting the others move on ahead of her.

She was alone. She looked at her watch. She had ten minutes precisely. Moving quickly but quietly, she went straight over to the index cupboard and inserted a skeleton key from her bag. She fiddled for a bit; then there was a click and the door came open. She took out the box labelled "C to D", shut the cupboard door and then hid herself under one of the sorting desks in the far corner of the room.

"Clindeuil...Clouseau...Clousette!" said Snippette to herself, as she pawed through the index cards. "Oh, Clousette again!...And another one!" There was no hedgehog listed by the name of Clou but there were three Clousettes. Snippette took out a piece of paper from her bag and began to scribble down the three addresses. Then she stopped, her eyes fixed on the door.

"Have you seen Snippette anywhere?" It was the supervisor's voice. She was standing at the door, looking into the room, but she did not look down and so did not see Snippette lurking in the shadows under the sorting desks.

"I think she must be in the toilette, madame," said another voice in the background.

"What? All this time?" queried the supervisor. "You'd better go and check she's all right." The supervisor turned around and left.

Snippette stopped trying to copy out the addresses. Instead she stuffed the three address cards in her bag and left the index box where it lay, on the floor under the desk. Then she opened the window and jumped out.

She landed in a small alley, where there was no one about to see her unusual exit. Straightening her skirt, she walked away as swiftly as she could without drawing attention to herself - out of the alley and into the main street. In her haste, she scarcely looked to left or right - until a screech of tyres made her stop and look up: she had almost got herself run over by a car full Hegemon officers.

One of the officers got out to see if she was all right and, before she could move, he had picked up her bag for her, which she had just dropped. She started thinking hard how she could explain away the index cards, but he had no reason to suspect her or search her bag. As he gave it back to her, he noticed the slight tremble of her paws but he assumed she was just in shock from having nearly been run over.

"Perhaps ve could give you a lift, *fräulein*?" said the officer. "You are in no state to valk."

Snippette looked at her watch: it was four minutes since the Post Office supervisor had remarked upon her absence and one minute since the end of the coffee break. She needed to get out of town quick, and a lift with the Hegemon officers was the lesser of two evils.

"Thank you - that's very kind," she responded. "If it isn't out of your way, I'm going to the Avenue des Pins on the other side of town."

The journey to the Avenue des Pins was uncomfortable, as the Hegemons tried to make polite conversation with Snippette. She tried hard to deflect the conversation away from herself; but in the end she could not prevent one of them from asking what she was going to do in the Avenue des Pins. She hesitated, then remembered there was a haberdashery there, so she said she was hoping to buy some cloth for a dress. Fortunately, the Hegemons did not appear to notice the hesitation. When at last they dropped Snippette off, she breathed an inward sigh of relief. And, as soon as the car had disappeared round the corner, she walked out of town - with no intention of ever going back.

Epine drove Snippette to the place where the first Clousette lived - a little village called Brouillet-les-Pistes. The door was opened by an elderly hedgehog, who looked as though she had been disturbed from her afternoon nap.

"Excuse me for disturbing you," began Snippette, "but are you Madame Clousette?"

"Yes, I am."

"Ah, good. My name's Snippette. I'd like to speak to your cousin, the Comte de Grif. May I come in? If he isn't here, I'm happy to wait."

"My cousin?" repeated the elderly hedgehog, looking puzzled. "But I don't have a cousin - and certainly not any Comte de Grif."

Snippette reckoned she was telling the truth, so Epine took her to the second address, a small farm called Tuchauffes. Epine stayed in the car while Snippette knocked at the door. After a few minutes, the door was opened by a young hoglet.

"Hallo there," said Snippette, smiling. "Is this Madame Clousette's house?"

"Er...yes," said the hoglet. "That's Mummy."

"And is Uncle Clou here?"

"No, he's -" the hoglet broke off as his mother appeared at the door.

"Who are you?" she asked a bit too suspiciously for her own good.

"My name's Snippette. I need to speak to your cousin, Clou. May I come in?"

Clousette looked at her hoglet and realized there was no point denying she had a cousin called Clou.

"What makes you think I know where he is?"

Snippette glanced behind her: they were alone and it was safe to talk - so long as she could trust Clousette, of course. You could never be sure but she had seen enough to take a chance on it.

"I'm a Bristlish agent," she explained. "I work for F.L.E.A. - the Field Liaison and Espionage Agency - and I've been sent here on a mission of vital importance. I urgently need Clou's help. We think he's gone to ground in the Clawdogne. You're his cousin and you live in the Clawdogne. It's not unreasonable to expect you should know where he is."

"Well, I don't," said Clousette. She tried to shut the door but Snippette blocked it with her foot.

"If you don't believe me, then listen to the wireless tonight at nine o'clock. Messages are read out after the news from Bristlin. Mine will be..." she hesitated a moment before continuing with a smile, "It'll be: *The flea market has come to town.*'"

"I don't have a wireless," said Clousette defensively.

Snippette shrugged her shoulders and walked away. The Hegemons might have banned wirelesses but everyone knew that there was scarcely a hedgehog in Furze who did not have access to one.

The following morning she returned, having arranged with F.L.E.A. H.Q. to have her message read out the previous night. This time Clousette let her in, though she still did not look particularly pleased to see her. Snippette noticed the hoglet she had met before and two others playing with toy aeroplanes on the living room floor. Clousette told them to go and play in the garden.

"So, you want to find my cousin. Why?" she asked.

"I'm afraid I can't tell you," said Snippette. "It's safer all round if as few hedgehogs as possible know about the mission; but it *is* very important."

"I'll see what I can do," said Clousette, opening the door to indicate that Snippette should leave. "If I find him, I'll let you know. But you mustn't come here again - I have a family to think of and I think that maybe you are a dangerous hedgehog to be around."

Snippette spent the next two days waiting to hear from Clousette. She heard nothing. It was six days altogether since she had parachuted into Furze and she had achieved nothing. How much longer could she afford to wait? She decided to give it one more day but then that was it. The day came and went, and still there was no news. It was now September the 1st. The invasion was planned for the 15th. With a feeling of intense disappointment, Snippette said goodbye to Hérisse, Epine and Grattain, and headed north.

* * *

When Snippette got off the train at Epiens in Prickardy, there was no one to meet her and no one she could go to. There was the family she had stayed with before the war, of course; but that was no good - it would just blow her cover and put the family in unnecessary danger. Beyond that she had no contacts in Prickardy - she had been relying on Clou for that. No contacts, no aerial photographs of the château - nothing.

She made her way into town alone, found herself a room in a hotel and radioed F.L.E.A. H.Q. to tell them her new whereabouts and see if they had any messages for her. They did. At last, some good luck! The invasion had been postponed until September the 27th, as the battle for control of the skies above Bristlin had not been going well for Hegemony. This gave Snippette an extra twelve days. Feeling considerably happier, she bought herself a bicycle and headed off for the Château Grif, which lay five miles to the south-west.

The château was a handsome brick building surrounded by a high wall and barbed wire. A single sentry stood guard by the gate but another paced up and down the road which ran alongside. Guards had also been posted in the towers which stood at either end of the front wall. Cycling past, Snippette briefly glimpsed the front of the building through the gate. It

was two storeys high - three in some places. No shutters were visible, so presumably they were on the inside; Snippette made a mental note. The front door was up a short flight of steps, either side of which was posted a sentry. Two officers were walking across the forecourt deep in conversation.

The high wall prevented Snippette from seeing anything more; and, as the wall now turned a corner and left the road behind, she was unable to check out even the perimeter of the estate any further without drawing attention to herself. With a sigh of frustration, she returned to her hotel.

As Snippette saw it, there were just two methods of getting into the château - by stealth or by invitation. They seemed equally impossible, so she decided to hedge her bets and plan for both: events would dictate which she used. Plan A would require a thorough recce of the château, which would have to be carried out later - under cover of darkness. Plan B required her to play the part of a collaborator - if possible, getting a job at the château, perhaps as a secretary or a cleaner.

She scoured the job ads in the local newspaper. There was nothing. Perhaps the Hegemons preferred not to advertise when selecting employees from a vanquished and hostile population. She abandoned the idea of a job at the château and instead went off to find the most expensive restaurant in town. This, she reasoned, was bound to be patronized by important Hegemon officers.

La Piquante was its name. It was the oldest and smartest restaurant in town - and very expensive. Snippette was told that there were no vacancies but did not let that put her off. By the time she had finished her piece, the manager was so impressed by her obvious knowledge of catering, her charm and her forged references, that he agreed to take her on anyway. She started the very same evening.

As she had expected, *La Piquante* was bristling with high-ranking Hegemon officers. Snippette went over to a table occupied by a general and a major.

"Good evening, *messieurs*. Are you ready to order?" she asked with a charming smile.

"Yes, I shall start viz *escargots à la bière*," said the general. "And, for ze main course, *raie à la priquardienne*."

"Certainly," said Snippette scribbling on her notepad. "And you, *monsieur*?"

She turned to look at the major and the smile froze on her face as, with a lurch of her stomach, she recognized Dornig, former-commandant of Gruntsey: whisked off Snippette's unimportant little island to higher things, no doubt.

"*Monsieur*?" she said, trying to look natural and praying that he would not recognize her; he had been a frequent enough visitor at her café, but surely he would not remember a mere waitress?

"I vill haf *escargots au vin* followed by *ommelette priquardienne* viz chips," said Dornig, with his nose in his menu. Snippette scribbled the order and was about to turn tail when he stopped her. "...and please ensure zat ze chips are vell cooked - I like my chips crisp."

Dornig looked her straight in the eye but showed no flicker of recognition. She nodded and, with an inward sigh of relief, made a hasty exit to the kitchen.

Snippette finished work at midnight. She had been on her feet for five hours and was utterly exhausted; but, instead of returning to the hotel and a warm bed, she cycled over to the wood which lay just to the north-east of the Château Grif. With a quick look behind her, she came off the road and hid her bicycle under a pile of leaves. Then she crept out of the wood and into the field adjoining the château's back wall.

Snippette approached the château on all fours, until her way was blocked by a barbed wire barrier. Just beyond the wire were a fast-running river and, a few feet further on, the castle wall.

There were still a few lights on at the château, mostly in the upper rooms; Snippette guessed that these would still be used as bedrooms - probably by the higher ranking officers. Making a quick sketch of the building, she marked down the windows which were lit and the ones which had been left open. Then, keeping low all the time, she crept along the wire fence to the point at which the river passed beneath it. Sliding into the water, she found a gap beneath the wire and came up on the other side. She then crawled up to the boundary wall to look for gaps or conveniently-placed trees. There were none.

She returned to the water, resubmerged and came up again just outside the wire.

"*Wer ist da*?" said a voice, which sounded halfway between aggression and fear.

Snippette slipped back under the water, as a torch was flicked on and its owner scanned the area with it. As soon as it was switched off again, Snippette came up for air, suppressing the urge to gasp. However, there was no sign of the Hegemon soldier, so she crawled up the bank and, though by now she had begun to shiver in her wet clothes and the cool night air, resumed her recce. For a few feet, it was more of the same; then a strange shape came into focus. She screwed up her eyes - an anti-aircraft gun, protected by a wall of sandbags. She moved away as silently as she could and, on reaching the wood, made a note of all she had seen.

It was nearly two in the morning when Snippette fell into her bed, flushed with excitement at the accomplishment of her first nocturnal recce. At long last, she had some sense of achievement. Morning brought her back to earth, however: the few details she had collected were in no way enough to make breaking into the château a realistic prospect. Perhaps there would be other opportunities to learn more; but, for the time being, she would have to concentrate on Plan B.

Over the next few days, she focussed all her energies on the job at the restaurant, trying to build up a relationship with the Hegemon officers who were regular customers there. To a certain extent, she was successful. They liked her and would always exchange a friendly word with her; but that was as far as it went. She was not going to get an invitation to the château on the basis of waiting at tables, however charming a waitress she might be. She would have to give events a helping paw.

The following afternoon, she cycled towards the Château Grif. She stopped just before the château came into view, turned her bicycle upside down and punctured the back wheel with a knife. Then she sat down and waited for the exodus of Hegemon officers heading off for the bright lights of Epiens at the end of their working day.

Before long, she caught the sound of a car approaching from the direction of the château. She got to her knees and pretended to examine the back wheel of her bicycle. The car came round the corner and she looked up. Major Dornig! Why did it have to be him of all hedgehogs?

Dornig saw her bending over her bicycle and, of course, stopped to see what was the matter.

"Mademoiselle Snippette, are you all right? You haf not an accident had?"

"Oh, nothing serious," said Snippette, rubbing her elbow. "I'm not hurt, but it looks as though I've got a puncture."

"Vhere vere you going?" he asked. "I vill give you a lift."

"Oh, that's most kind," said Snippette, as Dornig's driver put her bicycle in the boot of the car and she got into the back with Dornig.

"I was off to pick blackberries - for the restaurant," she said as she settled down beside him. "Would you like me to pick some for you?" she asked with another of her charming smiles.

"Very much," said Dornig, smiling back, "but only if you haf enough to spare."

"Oh, I've brought two large baskets with me, so there'll be more than enough for everyone," said Snippette. Then she looked at her watch with a little gasp: "Oh no! I had no idea it was so late, and I've got to be back at the restaurant at six forty-five. I must have lost more time than I realized with that puncture."

"Zen let me help you," said Dornig, graciously.

"Pick blackberries?"

"Vhy not? Many paws make light vork."

"But weren't you on your way somewhere?"

"Only to *La Piquante*," he said. "I am booked for dinner at seven and intended to arrive early for a smoke and a pre-dinner drink. But, after sitting behind a desk all ze day, I vould much prefer blackberries to pick."

Snippette took Dornig to a little bramble thicket nearby and together they filled the baskets, chatting as they worked. Snippette tried not to mention the war, so soon Dornig was asking her questions about her background. - Where had she grown up? Did she have brothers and sisters? The questions were innocent enough but it was the first time her cover story had been tested and she concentrated so hard that she hardly picked any blackberries at all. However, Dornig took his task very seriously and, within an hour, the baskets were full to overflowing. With time and blackberries to spare, they sat down on the grass to rest and feast.

"You know," said Dornig, looking her straight in the eye, "zere is somesing very familiar about you...I sink ve must haf met before."

"Oh, I don't think so" said Snippette casually, though her heart was thumping. "I'm sure I would have remembered - I have a good memory for faces."

"It vill come back to me," said Dornig confidently. "Perhaps you haf been to Hegemony?"

"No - never," said Snippette definitely.

"Hm, zen perhaps before ze -"

"I'm afraid I have to go now, Major," said Snippette looking at her watch.

"But of course," said Dornig, leaping to his feet. "I hope I haf not made you late."

"On the contrary," replied Snippette. "I could never have picked so many blackberries without you. Thank you so much for your help."

"It vas my pleasure. I haf not enjoyed myself so much since a long time. Perhaps..." he added, hesitating a little, "perhaps, if you are not already busy, you vould like to accompany me to ze officers' ball at ze château? - next veekend?"

"At the château?" repeated Snippette. "I'd love to." Her eyes lit up with real pleasure. After all the bad luck she had had so far, she could hardly believe her ears.

The following morning, before setting off for work, Snippette started to formulate a plan for the night of the ball. Somehow, she was going to have to slip away from the party unnoticed, work out where the invasion plans were stored, access and copy them and then escape - all without anyone noticing. It was more than a tall order: it was well-nigh impossible. The information she had gleaned from her night-time recce was woefully inadequate. But time and tide wait for no hedgehog, and she was unlikely to get another invitation to the château. So she decided to stake everything - her life and the lives of thousands of other hedgehogs - on this one chance.

Compiling a list of the things she would need to smuggle into the château, Snippette soon began to wonder whether her handbag would be big enough: the sketch from her recce, skeleton keys, camera, pistol, explosives and wire-cutters. But she was loath to do without any of these items, so she went out and bought herself the largest bag she thought she could get away with and, of course, a very nice dress for the ball.

Serving lunch at the restaurant was a welcome distraction, and Snippette concentrated all her attention on her customers. They were a different sort of bunch who came there at lunchtime - Furzish hedgehogs having business lunches and not so many Hegemon officers. But there was one hedgehog who struck her as rather out of place. He sat on his own at a corner table and, by the way he dressed, he did not look as though he could afford to eat there. Snippette was not at all surprised when he ordered the cheapest thing on the menu. She *was* surprised, however, when he put a note in her paw along with the money for the bill.

She took the note into the lavatory where she could read it unobserved:

Clou is here and wants to meet you. Meet me behind La Piquante at five o'clock and I will tell you where to find him.
- A Friend.

Snippette looked at the piece of paper in astonishment. She had given up her search for Clou as a lost cause when she came north; now he had turned up in the nick of time! If she could get a plan of the château from him, the odds would still be stacked against her but not as steeply as they were now. She wondered how he had known where to find her - only F.L.E.A. H.Q. were supposed to know her mission or whereabouts; a flicker of suspicion arose in her mind but she pushed it away - she had given the Hegemons no reason to suspect her and confided in no-one.

At five o'clock sharp, following her instructions, Snippette went out the back of *La Piquante*. There was no one there. She walked up the iron stairway to the little bridge that led over the canal and looked around for the stranger but there was still no sign of him - just a couple of Hegemon soldiers walking in her direction. She began to retreat back down the stairway but the soldiers walked past without taking any notice of her.

At five-fifteen, her hedgehog finally appeared: "Sorry I'm late. There was a road block on the way into town."

"You say you know where Clou is?" said Snippette, getting straight to the point.

"Yes, he's here in Prickardy, especially to see you. His cousin Clousette gave him your message, so he came north looking for you - at great personal risk to himself, I may say. You see, he's well known here and if the Hegemons get wind of his whereabouts they'll pull out all the stops to capture him. They know what he gets up to in his spare time, and, if they do capture him, he'll be shot. That's why I'm here - it's too dangerous for him to show his face in town."

"What *does* he get up to?"

"You don't know?" responded the stranger, somewhat taken aback. "He's the leader of an escape line - he helps prisoners-of-war on the run get back to Bristlin. I thought that was why you wanted to see him."

"No," said Snippette simply. "How did you know where to find me?"

"I'm in the local Resistance. I contacted F.L.E.A., explained that Clou was looking for you, and they told me you were working here."

"I see," said Snippette, smiling at the simplicity of his explanation - she wondered why she had been suspicious. "So, where do I find Clou?"

"He's hiding in a disused farmhouse in Aiguillers, a hamlet to the south-east of Epiens. He's in the last house on the left. Knock three times, wait and then knock once more."

"When's he expecting me?"

"You can turn up whenever you like - he's not going anywhere. But I'd urge you to go as soon as you can, all the same. Every day he spends here, his life is in jeopardy."

"Of course," said Snippette. "I'll go first thing tomorrow morning."

"Good. Well, I'd better be going. If you need me for anything, leave a message here - see, under this loose cobble. I pass by twice a day, on my way to and from work. If the cobble's upside down, I'll check it."

"Thank you - thank you for everything," said Snippette. She hesitated: "I'd like to be able to you explain to you why this all matters so very much..."

"That's all right," said the other. "We all have secrets to keep in this beastly war," he added as, with a wave of his paw, he disappeared down a back alley - and Snippette realized that he had never even told her his name.

Early the next morning, Snippette set off on her bicycle towards Aiguillers. The hamlet was as remote as anywhere in this well-populated corner of Furze but not remote enough to put her at her ease: on the way she passed two Hegemon cars, a Hegemon truck and a lorry. Fortunately, none of them showed any interest in her and she reached her destination without incident.

Aiguillers was a typical Prickardy hamlet, with its seven or eight low red-brick buildings clustered round a single street. There were few windows facing out into the street, which gave the place a curiously blank look, punctured only by the gated archways that led to inner courtyards or gardens. Snippette dismounted and looked around. The place was deathly quiet and crumbling into gentle decay. No one was looking - there *was* no one to look. She wheeled her bicycle along to the last house on the left and, letting herself in through the gate, found herself in a low, three-sided courtyard. To her left lay a large expanse of lawn, ending in a tiny patch of woodland and, beyond that, open fields.

She propped her bicycle against a wall and then knocked on the door three times. After a short pause, she knocked once more and waited. A few moments later, the door was opened by a male hedgehog of about her own age.

"Yes?"

"I'm Snippette."

"Good. I'm Clou. You'd better come in."

They shook paws, and Clou led Snippette into a ramshackle living room hidden beneath a thick layer of dust and cobwebs. A rifle lay on the table, alongside a dirty plate and glass of wine. Clou brushed off a chair for her.

"Did anyone see you come here?"

"No. I made sure I wasn't being followed when I left town, and there's no one out and about it in the village."

"There wouldn't be. It was abandoned in the last war. It was in the thick of the fighting, you see, and the hedgehogs who lived here never came back."

"And now we're at it again," said Snippette grimly.

"Indeed," said Clou with a nod of his head. "Well, how can I help you?"

Snippette paused. It was the first time she had confided in anyone and she had grown so used to operating alone that it seemed very unnatural.

"Well, as you no doubt realize," she said, drawing a deep breath, "the Hegemons are planning an invasion of Bristlin. What you may not know is that the invasion plans are being kept in the Château Grif. My mission is to find those plans and photograph them for the Bristlish government. The trouble is that I don't know which room they're kept in or, indeed, anything about the layout of the château. That's where you come in. I need you to draw me a plan of the château and help me work out an escape route."

Clou stared at her in astonishment. "But that's sheer madness! You can't just go wandering around the Château Grif - it'll be bristling with Hegemons. You won't get more than a few yards before you're caught. I won't have anything to do with it - I'd be helping you to commit suicide."

"The lives of thousands of Bristlish hedgehogs and maybe the outcome of the war depends upon this," said Snippette. "You risked your life coming here without even knowing why. Why shouldn't I risk mine when I know so much depends upon it?"

"Hm," said Clou, a frown creeping across his brow as a thought occurred to him. "I notice you didn't ask for my help to get *into* the château - only out. Do you already have a plan for getting in?"

"I have an invitation to the officers' ball at the weekend. I'm Major Dornig's guest."

"You're going with Major Dornig!" exclaimed Clou. "How...?" his voice tailed off into an embarrassed silence.

"He's a customer at *La Piquante*," explained Snippette. "I managed to engineer him into picking blackberries with me. We got friendly, and he invited me to the dance."

"You sound as though you liked him," said Clou.

"Well, he's pleasant company," said Snippette, shrugging her shoulders.

"Pleasant company!" repeated Clou with distaste. "I don't think you'd say that if *your* country had been occupied by Hegemony."

"It *has* been," retorted Snippette, needled by his accusation. "I'm from Gruntsey, and, in fact, Dornig used to be the commandant there."

"I'm sorry," said Clou. "I shouldn't have presumed... It's only that Dornig's the one who's after me - he's in charge of investigating the escape line. They say he's not bad as Hegemons go but, when it comes down to it, he's still fighting on the wrong side..."

"I know. That's why I'm doing this."

Clou smiled apologetically. "Look, I take it you never met Dornig while he was commandant?"

"Not socially, but he was a fairly frequent visitor to the café I worked at."

"You're playing a very dangerous game! What on earth possessed you to choose *him*?"

"I didn't. It was just chance. Anyway, he hasn't recognized me yet."

"Hm, let's hope your luck holds. - You're certainly going to need more than your fair share. I mean, you do realize, don't you, that getting into the château is only half the battle?"

"I'm only too well aware."

Clou fixed her with his piercing brown eyes: "I suppose you're hoping to slip away when the party gets into full swing and the rest of the château is deserted?"

"That's the general idea."

He smiled and leaned forward: "OK, so we need to work out for you the most likely location for the invasion plans. Do you have any paper?"

"Paper and pen," said Snippette, who had come fully prepared.

Clou began to sketch out a plan of the château for her - first the ground floor and then the first floor and even the cellars, for good measure: "I think it's the ground floor you'll be wanting. The first floor was just bedrooms in my day and I reckon it'll have stayed that way. The offices are probably all on the ground floor. The ballroom is clearly still a ballroom if they're holding a dance there. But I reckon it'll probably be one of the grander rooms you want. Who's the most senior officer there - do you know?"

"General Spitz."

"Well, it'll undoubtedly be General Spitz who's got the plans in his office. So we're looking for a room fit for a general. I reckon it'll be the library, the dining room or the drawing room."

"Or perhaps the billiard room?"

"Perhaps. But I'd try the other three first. Anyway, he won't be in the east wing - that's the servants' quarters."

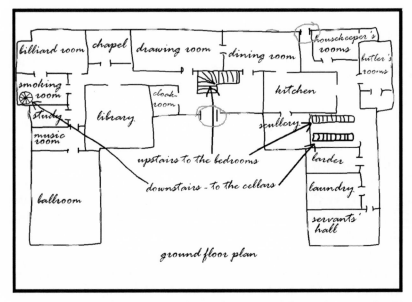

ground floor plan

"Thank you for this," said Snippette with real warmth. "I feel I'm really getting somewhere now."

"Well, don't forget it's only guesswork, and we haven't worked out your escape route yet." Clou began to sketch a plan of the château's grounds and surroundings. "I assume you've done a recce of the exterior?"

"Yes. There's one sentry guarding the entrance and another patrolling the road. There are also guards in the towers and by the front door and the whole place is surrounded by barbed wire. That's all I can tell you, I'm afraid. It's pretty limited, what you can see over a six foot wall."

"Well, that's something to work on all the same," said Clou. He sketched out a plan of the exterior; then Snippette marked with a cross where the sentries were posted.

"OK," said Clou, examining the sketch. "It looks as though there's a blind spot here," he said, indicating the area with a red scrawl.

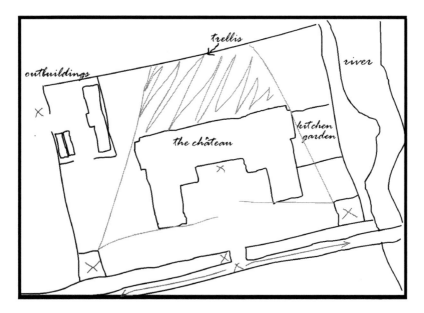

"But there's no way out there," said Snippette. "I won't be able to scale the boundary wall without a ladder."

"I think you will," said Clou. "Unless the Hegemons have pulled it down, there's a fairly sturdy trellis on the back wall. You can climb up that and jumped down the other side. You'll need wire-cutters for the barbed wire, of course."

"That's not a problem," said Snippette. "They'll fit into my bag a bit more easily than a ladder!"

Clou looked at Snippette: "You do realize, of course, that there may be more sentries inside the wall. You're taking quite a chance, relying on an external recce alone."

"Well, I suppose a Plan B wouldn't go amiss," responded Snippette. "Have you any - ?"

She stopped mid-sentence. Clou was holding up a paw for silence.

"What is it?" she whispered.

"I heard a car," said Clou, who had the sharpened hearing of a hunted hedgehog. He hurried over to a patch of wall which had been stripped of its plaster, removed a loose brick and looked through a makeshift peephole. "The Hegemons are here!" he said breathlessly. "We have to leave now. Quick - follow me! We can hide in the copse at the back." He slung his rifle over his shoulder and darted out of the door.

Snippette stuffed Clou's drawings in her bag and ran out after him, collecting her bike as she went. Clambering onto the saddle, she bumped her way across the lawn to the copse where Clou had already hidden himself. As she reached the trees, the farmhouse gate creaked behind her. She flung her bicycle to the ground and dropped behind a bush alongside Clou. Seconds later, a group of Hegemon soldiers stormed into the courtyard, followed by their officer.

"*Feldwebel*," called out the officer, "*suchen Sie ihn im Hause. Wir bleiben im Garten.*" Several of the soldiers disappeared into the house but the others remained, sniffing around the courtyard.

Snippette eyed the officer. She knew that voice - "Dornig!" she exclaimed in a whisper. "If he sees me here it's all over!"

Clou glanced at her with a wry smile: "It's a shame I can't just shoot him but I suppose you'd have no one to take you to the ball then."

Dornig was starting to walk towards them, flanked by two hedgehogs with machine guns. Snippette remembered how thorough he had been at his blackberry picking and reckoned it was only a matter of time before he discovered them.

"You'd better go before it's too late," whispered Clou. "I'll cover you. Whatever you do, don't look round. - And, don't worry, I won't hurt him."

Snippette looked at Clou. Every fibre of her being rebelled against the idea of leaving him behind. He could not hold out for more than a few minutes when he was so greatly outnumbered - the Hegemons would win paws down. To leave Clou would be shabby and unheroic. Yet Snippette knew that she must: the lives of thousands of hedgehogs depended upon her surviving to fight another day. She put a paw on his shoulder but could not find the words to express what she felt.

"Don't feel bad," said Clou, with a wistful smile. "I've always known it might come to this. It's the right thing to do." He aimed his rifle in the direction of the farmhouse and squeezed the trigger gently with his paw. "Ready?"

Snippette nodded.

"Go!"

Clou opened fire. Snippette jumped up onto her bicycle and rode away from the battle as fast as she could. Several bullets hit the ground to the right and left of her but she took no notice until a sudden sharp pain made her look down: blood was streaming down her leg where a bullet had gone clean through it. Gasping with agony she rode on, and gradually the noise of the gunfire retreated. Eventually she reached a road. She hesitated, wondering whether to take it - it would be far quicker but there was a much greater risk of meeting Hegemon troops along the way. The next thing she knew, a motorcycle had appeared around the corner. She made a move towards the bushes but it was too late. The motorcycle screeched to a halt beside her.

"You'd better get on," said the rider. It was the hedgehog from the local Resistance.

Breathing a sigh of relief, Snippette hid her bicycle among some bushes and climbed onto the back of the motorcycle. A few minutes later, they were safe at his home in a neighbouring village.

"What happened to Clou?" he asked when he had finished bandaging her leg.

Snippette steeled herself to tell the truth. "I had to leave him. I couldn't afford to be caught. It's my mission - it's just too important."

He looked at her accusingly but said nothing. He knew perfectly well that sacrifices had to be made but Clou was his friend and his abandonment by Snippette was hard to stomach. He had no idea what this mission of hers was. Was it really so vital? Or did she just have an over-inflated ego?

"You'd better stay here for a few days while your leg mends," he said. "You can use my phone - tell the restaurant that you're ill."

"Thank you, I'll stay here tomorrow but after that I have to go."

"If you go out with that leg of yours, you're a fool. Even if you wear trousers to cover up the wound, that limp will still give you away before you've walked two paces. - And, whatever this precious mission of yours is, Clou's sacrifice will have been for nothing," he said pointedly.

Snippette swallowed hard and looked away. She had conquered her fear but nothing had prepared her for this. Why had she accepted this accursed mission? The Allies needed hedgehogs like Clou if they were to win the war. Yet his life had been practically thrown away and it was her fault. Of course, the answer was simple enough: the invasion had to be stopped. If Bristlin fell, the war would be lost and thousands more lives destroyed.

Snippette looked her accuser in the eye.

"I won't limp," she said emphatically.

* * *

Sunday arrived - the day of the ball. Dornig collected Snippette at seven o'clock sharp and took her to the Château Grif in his chauffeur-driven car. As they swept up the drive, she forgot the near impossibility of her mission. It was the moment she had been working for all these long hard weeks, and her spines tingled with excitement.

"Vell, here ve are," said Dornig, as they walked up the steps.

"Here we are indeed," agreed Snippette, wincing slightly.

Dornig frowned. "Are you all right?"

"I'm fine. I'm just not used to high heels," she explained, putting her full weight on her wounded leg and smiling through the pain.

Dornig took her into the ballroom, which was already bristling with Hegemon officers and their guests. It was much more glamorous than anything Snippette had ever been to before but, with the money she had been given for her mission, she had been able to buy a very elegant dress. In fact, she was one of the best-dressed hedgehogs there, and it was not only Dornig who noticed her. Soon the other officers were swarming around her like fleas. Eventually even General Spitz himself asked to be introduced to her. The other officers melted away.

"You haf all your life in Prickardy lived, Fraülein Snippette?" asked Spitz.

"No, I'm from the south. I came to Prickardy to study the regional cuisine."

"Ah yes, I hear zat you vork at *La Piquante*. A very fine - "

"Excuse me, Herr General," interrupted a soldier, rushing into the room with an envelope in his paw. "Zere is an urgent message for Major Dornig."

Dornig opened the letter and passed it to Spitz: "A new prisoner has just been transferred here, Herr General. In view of ze circumstances, I must see him immediately. You may vish to be present?"

Spitz read the letter and nodded his agreement. "You must excuse us, Fraülein Snippette. Urgent business calls us avay."

Dornig kissed Snippette's paw, "I am very sorry, Mademoiselle Snippette. I shall be as qvick as possible."

"Please don't hurry on my account," said Snippette, who really meant it. "I shall be fine."

Dornig nodded his head and clicked his heels. Then he left the room with General Spitz, and the two officers hurried downstairs to the cell where the prisoner was being held. As the cell door clunked shut behind them, the prisoner slowly got to his feet.

"Good evening, Flight Lieutenant Spike," said Dornig. "Velcome to ze Château Grif. I believe you haf a particular interest in ze Château Grif?"

"Why have I been brought here?" demanded Spike, looking from Dornig to Spitz. "You've no right to question me. I'm a member of His Majesty's Air Force - not some spy you've uncovered."

Spitz said nothing. This was Dornig's show.

"Come now, Flight Lieutenant," said Dornig. "You can hardly expect us to ignore ze fact zat you haf been photographing our château." He smiled. "Vhat vas ze purpose of your mission?"

"You have my name, rank and number. That's all you need to know," said Spike defiantly. "I demand to be taken to a prisoner-of-war camp!"

"You vill be - in due course," responded Dornig with a charming smile. "Now, tell me - are ze Bristlish intending to bomb us? Perhaps zat is vhy you are so keen to go to a camp?"

"Look, I don't know the purpose of my mission. I didn't need to know, so they didn't tell me." Spike sat down and stared intently at the wall.

Dornig fixed him with a piercing stare, trying to work out whether he was telling the truth: he decided not to give him the benefit of the doubt. "Come, come, Flight Lieutenant," said Dornig. "Do you really expect me to believe zat?...Vell, I am a patient hedgehog. I can vait." He leant back against the wall and lit a cigarette. "Do you smoke, Flight Lieutenant?" he asked, offering the packet to him.

Spike hesitated and then nodded. He had not had a cigarette since his capture and that was days ago now. He took one to smoke in peace after Dornig and Spitz had gone.

As he put it away, he knocked a photograph out of his pocket. Dornig bent down to pick up the photograph and was about to return it to Spike but suddenly stopped in his tracks. The picture was of Snippette.

"Your vife?" asked Dornig as casually as he could.

"My sister."

"She is very pretty."

"Is she?" responded Spike in typical brotherly fashion.

"Vhat is her name?"

Spike hesitated for a moment but could see no harm in giving his sister's name. "Snippette," he replied, little knowing the significance of what he said.

Dornig returned the photograph to Spike and then turned to Spitz: "Herr General, if you vill excuse me, zere is somesing I must see to..."

Without waiting for a reply, he left the cell. Spitz and Spike were alone. The general was slightly taken aback by Dornig's sudden departure but he was not sorry to see him go. In his opinion, Dornig was far too soft with prisoners. He stepped forward and eyed Spike through his monocle: "Ze major has been gentle viz you because of his respect for ze Bristlish armed forces. I regretfully am not so professionally understanding... So, you vill tell me now ze purpose of your mission."

It was a statement, not a question, but Spike just stared at the wall in silence.

"It vill be better for you if you tell me now," said Spitz, raising his voice slightly. "I *vill* get zis information from you sooner or later."

Spike continued to stare at the wall.

"Ve haf vays of making you talk!"

* * *

Snippette slipped away from the ballroom at the first opportunity. Removing her shoes, she crept painfully but silently along the deserted corridor towards the room which had been Clou's library. There she knocked at the door and, hearing no answer, unpicked the lock. However, as soon as she stepped inside, she turned around again: there were four desks in this room, and she felt sure Spitz would have an office all to himself. She proceeded down the hallway to the drawing room.

This time she was in luck: there was just one desk, and on it was a pile of letters addressed to Spitz. She flicked through them and then checked the drawers but there was nothing of any interest. She was going to have to open the safe. This was a large and robust-looking metal cabinet; it was certainly no lock-picking job. So, taking the plastic explosive out of her bag, she pressed it into and around the lock, and attached the detonator and a short fuse. Then she lit the fuse, ran to the far end of the room - as fast as her leg would allow her - and curled up in a ball behind the sofa.

"Phoomp!" The safe door blew open in a cloud of smoke.

Snippette limped back to the safe and hurriedly began to search inside it. Every second counted. Dornig might be back at the party by now, wondering where she had got to; and, if anyone had heard the explosion above the sound of the band, they would be on their way to investigate right now.

Sifting through Spitz's papers at lightning speed, she allowed herself to be distracted momentarily when she came across the aerial reconnaissance photographs of the Château Grif - the photographs which had been meant for her! She stuffed the photographs in her bag and carried on her search.

And there, at last, it was - a folder entitled *Unternehmen Seeigel*, which meant *Operation Sea Urchin*. This was the codename for the planned invasion of Bristlin. Inside the folder were lists of troops and equipment, detailed orders and a spine-chilling map illustrating how Hegemony planned to sweep up through southern Bristlin. Snippette put the plans in her bag. There was no point photographing them - not with the door of the safe blown open. The Hegemons would know she had been there and seen the plans. Now she had to make good her escape.

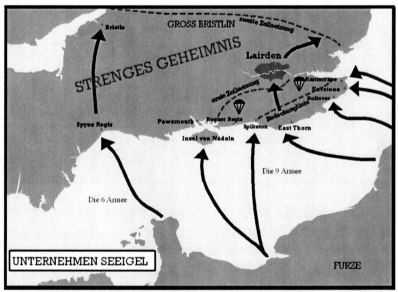

Snippette consulted Clou's sketch of the château. The exit she was after was in the servants' quarters in the east wing. It was a stone's throw from the cellars, and her thoughts were drawn irresistibly to Dornig's prisoner, who she was sure would be held there. She knew she ought to get out of the château straight away. Her first duty was to get the invasion plans safely back to Bristlin. The prisoner was not her concern and she had no right to jeopardize the mission. And yet... And yet, whoever this prisoner was, he was important enough to drag both Dornig and Spitz away from the ball.

Snippette opened the door a crack and peeped out. The corridor was empty and distant music the only sound. She picked up her bag and hobbled through the hallway to the servants' quarters and down the stairs to the cellars. At the same moment, Dornig ascended the stairs on the far side of the château.

Dornig muttered to himself as he hurried up the stairs to the ballroom. He had been sure he had met Snippette somewhere before. Now he knew where. Spike's photograph of Snippette had been taken in St Pricklier's Port, the capital of Gruntsey. Dornig remembered her clearly now - the pretty waitress in the seafront café. He had tried to be friendly once or twice but she had been very prickly; and just a few weeks into the occupation, she had disappeared. Now she had turned up in Prickardy, pretending to be Furzish. What she was after, he had yet to work out; but of one thing he was sure: Snippette was a Bristlish spy.

Dornig hurried into the ballroom and pushed his way through the throng of guests, looking for Snippette. She was nowhere to be found. He asked around but no one had seen her for a while. He would have to search the building. He rushed to his own office but there was no sign that she had been there. So he tried the others. They were all locked except for General Spitz's office. Flinging the door open, he rushed in with a gun in his paw. She was not there. But the door of the safe hung open and on the floor was a pair of high-heeled shoes - Snippette's shoes - the ones she had complained about as they arrived at the château. In her hurry to leave, she had left them behind.

Snippette realized her mistake as she padded along the cold floor of the cellar but it mattered little. Dornig would be on to her by now anyway. She hurried past the coal store and the tool room towards the end of the corridor. Taking her pistol out of her bag, she peered round the corner. A guard was sitting at a table playing solitaire. She crept up behind him and pressed the gun against his back.

"Don't breathe a word or I'll shoot," she whispered, her voice as hard as nails. He dropped his cards and put his paws up. "Now get up very slowly and put your rifle on the table. Good. Now let the prisoner out."

"Vhich prisoner?" asked the guard nervously.

"All of them!" said Snippette, a little alarmed. She had not expected more than the one prisoner - the château was an army H.Q., after all - not a prison. However, she had no intention of leaving anyone behind now.

The guard unlocked the first cell. A tired and slightly bemused-looking Clou walked out. So he was alive after all! Repressing the strong feelings she felt on seeing him again, Snippette simply nodded towards the rifle on the table. It took him a moment to take the situation in but, when he saw Snippette, he smiled with profound relief.

"Have you got what you came for?" he asked, as he picked the rifle up.

Snippette nodded again. "Yes, but I had to blow the safe open, and Dornig's bound to be looking for me by now. We've very little time."

"You shouldn't have - " began Clou, but Snippette had stopped listening. General Spitz had emerged from the second cell with his paws up. Behind him came her brother Spike.

"Spike!" exclaimed Snippette, unable to believe her eyes.

"Snippette!" exclaimed Spike, who was even more surprised to see her.

Clou vaguely noticed the resemblance between the two of them but his mind was on other things. Taking the keys off the guard, he locked the two Hegemons in the cells. Then he turned to Snippette and Spike. "Right," he said. "Let's get out of here."

"Not quite yet," said Snippette, coming back to earth. "I've got some aerial reconnaissance photographs of the Château Grif. I think we should have a look at them before we go."

Clou wondered how this extraordinary hedgehog had managed to get her paws on these photographs. However, it was no time for a question and answer session. "Very well," he said, "but it had better be quick."

Snippette spread the photographs out on the table, and Clou flicked through them. "Well, the trellis is still there," he said, "and there don't seem to be any extra guards at the back of the house. Good. It looks as though our escape route is sound. Let's go."

"Hold on a minute," said Spike. "Am I right in thinking that you're planning to go over the back wall? Only there's something funny going on here, between the wall and the wire."

"What do you mean?" asked Snippette. "I can't see anything. It's just grass."

"Yes, but look how it changes colour. The earth has been disturbed here. I'd say the place was mined... I do know what I'm talking about: it was me that took the photographs."

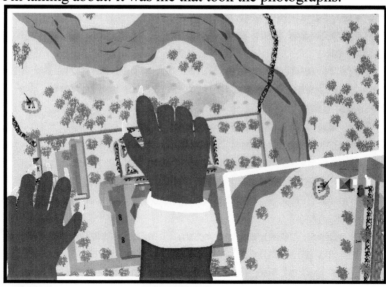

Snippette stared at Spike and then the photograph "So the recce I did that night...?"

"You must have been very lucky," said Clou.

"How about a Plan B?" asked Snippette gravely.

Clou pondered for a moment. "There may be another way. There's an old well in the basement, which used to be fed by the river via an underground channel. It's dry now - it hasn't been used in years - but it's risky. The entrance is definitely big enough for us but, as for the rest, I just don't know. As you might expect, I've never been in it."

"Well, there aren't any alternatives, are there?" said Snippette. "So, do we all agree?"

They did. Clou took them to the well and, after rummaging around in a corner of the cellars which had been left untouched by the Hegemons, he found a length of rope. He tied the rope to the spindle which had formerly held the water bucket and, one by one, the three hedgehogs slid down to the bottom of the well.

"Which way?" asked Snippette. There were two tunnel entrances, one slightly higher than the other.

"They both connect with the river," said Clou. "The water used to come in through here and the overflow went out the other way. We'll take this one. It comes out near the woods."

He clambered up into the higher of the two tunnel entrances and the others followed. It was dark, airless and slightly slippery in the tunnel - and too low to stand. They stayed on all fours and crawled.

Above them, a thorough search of the château was in full swing. Failing to find Snippette himself, Dornig had finally alerted the guards and was about to explain the situation to General Spitz. He had been dreading this moment - he was, after all, responsible for bringing Snippette into the château; but he could not put it off any longer. He headed down to the basement.

Snippette and her companions were by now halfway to the river. The tunnel had got smaller and smaller until their heads scratched the ceiling but at last they could see the light at the end of the tunnel.

Clou paused to brief the others: "When we get to the river, we head left and follow the river bank to the wire. Keep your heads down and you shouldn't be visible."

A few minutes later and they were there. As they emerged into the twilight by the river, there was a deceptive peacefulness about the place. Dornig had doubled the guards at the exits and the search of the château was going on but outside the château walls all was quiet. Keeping down on all fours, they crawled along the muddy bank towards the wire. As they neared it, they heard voices. Snippette remembered the anti-aircraft gunners she had encountered on her night-time recce and signalled to the others to keep moving. As long as they were quiet, the gunners would stay at their post; they were watching the sky - not the riverbank.

When they finally reached the perimeter fence, Snippette went to the front of the line and began to make an opening in the barbed wire with the wire-cutters from her bag. It was slow work and she was only halfway through when...

"*Feldwebel! Feldwebel! Suchen Sie dem Umkreiszaun entlang!*"

It was Dornig's voice. He was shouting from some way off but his words sent a shiver down Snippette's spines: he had just ordered his hedgehogs to search the perimeter fence. Snippette worked frantically now: snip...snip...cutting through the wires one by one - and then, at last, she was through. She turned round and raised a paw to beckon the others forward but then suddenly froze.

Someone was running in their direction. The stomp of his boots was getting closer and closer but stopped a short distance away from them. There was silence - just the sound of his breathing. Snippette willed him to go away, and he did begin to move; but he was coming in their direction. Snippette reached into her bag for her gun.

Suddenly all hell broke loose - a gun battle had started up somewhere over towards the château. Snippette did not stop to wonder what was going on. The guard had turned back and was running towards the fighting. She beckoned the others forward and, one by one, they crawled through the opening in the barbed wire and continued along the river, towards the woods.

As soon as they reached the trees, they climbed up the bank of the river and ran as fast as they could, away from the château. Clou led the way but, in his weakened state, stumbled. Spike helped him up. "Are you all - ?" began Snippette, limping up behind them.

"Ssh!" said Clou. "I heard something."

A twig snapped just a few feet away. Thrusting her paw into her bag, Snippette swivelled round, just as a hedgehog stepped out from behind a tree.

"Hey, don't shoot!" he said, with a smile. "It's only me!" It was the mysterious hedgehog from the Furzish Resistance.

"You!" said Snippette, hastily putting her pistol away.

"Piques!" exclaimed Clou, who had joined them now. "What on earth...?"

"Never mind that now," said Piques, though it was clear that he was mightily glad to see Clou. "So, is it just the three of you?"

"That's right," said Clou.

"Good. You'll fit into my van then. Now, listen carefully - I'll say this only once. You need to carry on due north for about five minutes. When you come to a dirt track, veer left - keep on going alongside the track and you'll find the van. Wait for me there. I've got to go back to the gang to let them know what's happening, but I'll catch you up."

Without another word, he turned tail and ran off in the opposite direction. Snippette, Clou and Spike carried on due north, where they found the van parked along a dirt track. A few minutes later, Piques rejoined them and drove them to a safe-house some thirty miles away. A hedgehog called Barbette was waiting for them by the front door.

"Three of them!" exclaimed Barbette. "I thought it was just Clou we were expecting. What are we going to do about identity papers?"

"You don't need to worry about me," said Snippette. "I've a spare of my own, but Spike..."

"That's all right," said Piques. "We've got some blanks. I'll take Spike's photograph and make up his papers. Meanwhile, Barbette, if could you look after them... They've had a rough time."

Barbette gave them all a change of clothes and then took them to the kitchen for a meal. Piques joined them a little later.

"So what were you doing at the château?" asked Clou, bolting his food down.

"Well, funnily enough, we'd come to rescue you," said Piques. "Me and the gang. We got news that you were being held at the château and so we decided to break in and get you. Not a high probability of success, I know, but we could hardly stand idly by."

"Dornig was OK," said Clou, shrugging his shoulders. "I could have done with more sleep and more to eat, but he never laid a paw on me."

Piques shook his head: "Dornig may have treated you relatively well but, sooner or later, he would have had to pass you over to the police. And we all know the penalty for helping prisoners-of-war to escape. There are no two ways about it: you would have been shot." He paused and smiled. "Of course, if I'd known that Snippette was staging a break-out of her own..."

"Actually, you turned up in the nick of time," said Snippette, looking up from her meal. "One of Dornig's hedgehogs was on the verge of finding us. Your attack drew him away."

"Well, I'm pleased to have been of service," replied Piques with a smile. Then he looked at his watch and his smile disappeared. "Look, you'd better all of you catch some sleep while you can. I'm going to have to move you on early in the morning. The Hegemons will soon be combing the area for you. We're going to take you south - over the Prickly Knee Mountains and across the border to Espina - you know, Clou, the usual route. Barbette will accompany you on the first leg."

Snippette looked at Piques. "You took over Clou's escape line?"

"That's right. Funny, isn't it, how we've been working together but neither of us has really known what the other was up to? - Actually, I still don't know exactly what it is you've been up to."

Snippette smiled. "Look, I'm really grateful for all your help but I can't go to Espina. It'll take too long - I've got to get back to Bristlin without delay. I'll radio F.L.E.A. H.Q. and ask them to send a plane."

"All right," said Piques, "but they won't be able to land a plane anywhere round here. The whole of northern Furze is bristling with Hegemon troops right now."

Barbette fetched a map and unfolded it on the table. "How about down here, near Pointiers?" she suggested. "I've got a contact there who could help."

"Pointiers?" repeated Snippette. "That's still quite a long way. Isn't there somewhere nearer?"

"Nearer!" exclaimed Piques. "Have you got some sort of death wish? I mean, you do know that they're building up for an invasion of Bristlin, don't you?"

"Yes, I'm well aware of that," said Snippette, and her thoughts travelled to the Top Secret invasion plans hidden in her bag. "If necessary I'll have to take the risk. The others can go over the Prickly Knee Mountains, as you suggest, but I really can't afford to hang around."

"Very well," sighed Piques, taking another look at the map, "but we *have* to steer clear of the coast. What about here, outside Pince? Is that near enough for you?"

"Yes, that's near enough," nodded Snippette. "Thank you."

"Right," said Spike. "I'll take the plane with Snippette. I've been itching to get back in the air." He did not mention that he did not want his sister to travel alone.

"I'll head south," said Clou, "but not to Espina. I'll go back to my cousin Clousette and join the local Resistance."

"So, that's settled then," said Piques. "Barbette, you take Clou south in the morning. I'll take Snippette and Spike to the plane. Now, it's about time everyone got some sleep. Clou, you'd better say your goodbyes - you've got an early start."

Clou shook paws with his old friend and with Spike. Then he went over to say goodbye to Snippette.

"It's been quite an experience, knowing you," said Clou. "I'll miss you."

"You should come back to Bristlin with us," urged Snippette. "It isn't too late. I'm sure there'd be a place for you in F.L.E.A.. You're just the sort of hedgehog they're looking for."

"Perhaps," responded Clou with a wistful shrug of his shoulders, "but my place is here, in my own country, fighting alongside my compatriots. Perhaps I could look you up after the war?"

"I'd like that," said Snippette earnestly.

"I'll need to know your real name," he said, fixing her with his piercing brown eyes.

"Snippette."

"I'm glad," replied Clou. "I've grown attached to it."

Clou kissed her on both cheeks, as was the Furzish custom, then went upstairs to bed.

* * *

Twenty-four hours later, Snippette, Spike and Piques stood in a secluded field thirty miles to the south-west of Epiens. It was two o'clock in the morning and the drone of the approaching aeroplane could just be heard. Two lines of hedgehogs - Piques' gang - stood in the middle of the field with their torches switched on to guide the plane down.

"Well, I suppose this is where we say goodbye," said Piques, extending a paw to Spike.

Spike shook the proffered paw warmly: "Thank you for everything you've done for us. I know the kind of risks you run."

"Yes, thank you," said Snippette, in turn. She looked at Piques hesitantly for a moment but then spoke again: "Look, I know you've wondered about my mission - whether it really is as important as I've made out. I've seen it in your face. Well I..." - she hesitated - "...I give you my word it is."

The plane was descending towards the field now, its twin engines getting louder and louder so that no one heard the end of Snippette's sentence. Spike turned to watch the plane land and taxi round in preparation for take-off.

"You don't have to say anything, Snippette," said Piques, shouting to be heard above the noise of the plane. "It's true I did wonder. Clou's a good friend and, when he was captured, well, to be honest, you didn't seem to care. But you risked your life to rescue him, didn't you? I mean, getting Clou out of the château wasn't part of your mission, was it?"

Snippette shrugged her shoulders and smiled. Rescuing Clou had not been part of the mission and went against her training but, had she left the château on her own, she would never have made it out alive. The truth was, she had needed Clou and Spike just as much as they had needed her.

Snippette and Piques embraced in the Furzish manner. Then Snippette tapped Spike on the shoulder: "Time to go!" she shouted.

Spike nodded, and Piques watched the two hedgehogs run off towards the waiting plane.

* * *

The journey home was happily an uneventful one, and they arrived back on the south coast of Bristlin safe and sound. Spike flew them on to his own station in north Lairden. Then they parted, and Snippette headed off into town to report to F.L.E.A. H.Q..

As she emerged from the underground, dawn was just breaking. The soft September sun tinged the sky a pinkish yellow. Below was a scene of devastation. The city had been bombed in Snippette's absence, in preparation for the planned invasion. She had heard about it in Furze but the reality was more shocking than she could have imagined. There was damage everywhere - shattered windows, holes blasted through walls and, here and there, whole houses reduced to a pile of rubble.

Sharpesbury Avenue had not escaped the bombs. As she picked her way through the debris, Snippette wondered whether No. 103 would still be there. Happily, it was - damaged, its roof partly open to the sky, but still standing. She went up the short flight of steps and let herself into the large entrance hall, in the middle of which sat the same uniformed hedgehog as on her previous visit.

"Good morning. I've come to see Brigadier Scrape. It's Snippette."

"Ah, yes. The brigadier's been expecting you. Please go up. You'll find him in room 5 - first floor, third door on the left."

Snippette made her way upstairs and knocked on the brigadier's door.

"Enter!" came the clipped, military voice.

Snippette entered. Brigadier Scrape was sitting with his feet up on the desk, staring at the gaping hole in his ceiling.

Snippette coughed. "It's me, sir," she said.

Scrape wrenched his attention away from the ceiling and jumped to his feet. "Ah, Snippette! Welcome back! How was it?"

"I got the invasion plans. Here they are," said Snippette breathlessly, scarcely able to believe her own words. She took the folder out of her bag and offered it to Scrape.

"Jolly good. You must tell me all about it," responded Scrape, but his paws remained in his pockets.

"Aren't you going to look at them, sir?" asked Snippette, stunned by Scrape's apparent lack of interest.

"No need," said Scrape. "No need now. The invasion's off."

"The invasion's off?" repeated Snippette, flabbergasted. "But I risked my life for this! - And Clou and Piques, my brother Spike...and *many* others..."

"But of course," said Scrape. "The point is that the Hegemons *know* we've got the invasion plans. They've lost the element of surprise. That's why they've cancelled the invasion. My dear Snippette, it's all because of you."

The End

Post-Script: Historical Note on "Where Hedgehogs Dare"

World War II

The war in which Snippette carried out her courageous mission bears a striking resemblance to the human conflict known as the Second World War (1939-1945). This started as a result of German aggression under the dictator, Adolf Hitler. Hitler wanted to unite all German-speaking peoples and dominate Europe. As a result, between 1939 and 1940, Germany invaded Czechoslovakia, Poland, Denmark, Norway, the Netherlands, Belgium and France; German-speaking Austria was incorporated into a "Greater Germany".

Great Britain Stands Alone

With the surrender of France, Great Britain[1] effectively stood alone against the might of Germany and its partners[2]. Hitler hoped and expected that Britain would surrender. However, under the determined leadership of its Prime Minister, Winston Churchill, Britain stood firm.

The Channel Islands

Between German-occupied France and Great Britain lie the Channel Islands. The Channel Islands are a dependency of the British monarchy and, though internally self-governing, rely upon Great Britain for their defence. However, in 1940, Britain's situation was desperate and the British government decided that they could not afford to defend the Channel

---

[1] Properly known as the "United Kingdom of Great Britain and Northern Ireland". Today we usually shorten this to the "United Kingdom". In those days, people usually referred to "Great Britain".

[2] The United States of America would not enter the war until December 1941. On Germany's side at this time were Italy, Russia and Hungary. Russia and Italy both later changed sides.

Islands, which were of no military importance. Instead, ships were sent so that the islanders could leave if they wanted to.

On 28th June 1940, the Luftwaffe (German air force) bombed the islands, killing 44 people. On 30th June, the island of Guernsey was occupied. The occupation of Jersey, Alderney and Sark followed - on 1st, 2nd and 4th July, respectively. Active resistance against the occupation was impracticable. The islands were too small and gave would-be resistance fighters nowhere to hide; the islanders were also very few (many of the men of military age had already left) while the German occupying force was disproportionately large. Liberation did not come until the end of the war in May 1945.

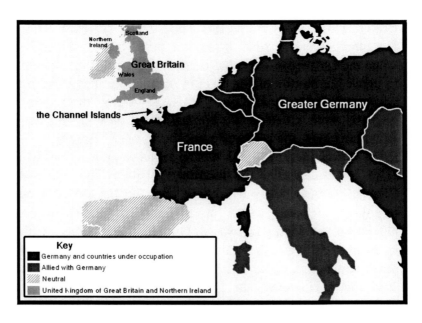

Operation Sea Lion and the Battle of Britain

When Churchill refused to negotiate a peace with Hitler, Hitler ordered his generals to plan the invasion of Britain - codenamed Operation Sea Lion and scheduled to take place in September. In the first version of the plan (there were several), German troops were to land by sea along a wide front stretching from Dorset in the south-west of England to Kent in the south-east. However, this was soon seen as unmanageable and the proposed front was narrowed so that the most westerly landing point would be in West Sussex. The initial assault was now to be conducted along a 45 mile stretch of coast by 60,000 men - mostly infantry, supported by about 250 tanks and limited artillery. Parachute troops would also be dropped in support. Once beachheads had been established, the first wave of troops was to fan out and join up to form a more continuous landing zone for the next wave. The German army would then push north, taking London as they went. The total invasion force was to number 160,000 men.

This invasion was to be preceded by a battle for the skies, between Germany's Luftwaffe and Britain's RAF (Royal Air Force) - the battle which came to be known as the Battle of Britain. Hitler thought that this battle would be easily won. In fact, there were terrible losses on both sides. Furthermore, when the Luftwaffe started to bomb British cities in an attempt to break the morale of the civilian population, they effectively weakened their attack on the RAF. Many thousands of civilians were killed in the bombardment now known as the Blitz. However, the Luftwaffe lost the Battle of Britain.

On 17th September 1940, having failed to gain control of the skies, Hitler cancelled the invasion of Britain. The tides in the Channel would shortly be against him and his thoughts were turning to Russia, which he planned to invade instead[3]. Operation Sea Lion gave way to Operation Barbarossa. Unlike in Snippette's story, the plans for the invasion of Britain were never stolen and, as far as I know, there was never any plan to steal them. However, the British did have agents operating undercover behind enemy lines.

---

[3] This was despite the fact that Russia and Germany were not at war with one another at the time. In fact, in 1939, they had signed a non-aggression treaty called the Molotov-Ribbentrop Pact. However, Hitler had long had designs on Russia in order to provide "living room" for the German people.

Special Operations Executive (S.O.E.)

S.O.E., which was set up in 1940 for the purpose of espionage and sabotage behind enemy lines, is probably the organization most famous for this type of activity during World War II. Its agents were given commando and parachute training and also specialist training - such as in demolition techniques or morse telegraphy. They were then sent on operations throughout occupied Europe. There they met with mixed success and their relations with local resistance movements and with other British intelligence organizations were not always good. However, they did have their successes and were extremely brave.

S.O.E. agents came from a variety of backgrounds (civilian as well as military) and also employed many women - in all, there were 3,200 women and 10,000 men. The principal qualification was a very good knowledge of the relevant country and, in particular, its language. Many of the agents had dual nationality.

France did not receive its first S.O.E. agent until May 1941 - after the Battle of Britain. However, during the course of the war and up until the liberation of France in August 1944, 400 men and 39 women were sent by F Section[4]. Of these, 91 men and 13 women did not return.

S.O.E. was officially dissolved in 1946.

The French Resistance

The French Resistance is the collective name given to those French citizens who actively resisted the German occupation during the war. It included small armed groups who engaged in sabotage and guerilla warfare, networks to help escaped prisoners-of-war and publishers of underground newspapers. No one knows how many men and women took part in the French Resistance except that they numbered in their

---

[4] The section under British control. The French had their own section - RF Section - which sent about the same number of agents.

thousands. They all ran the risk of being shot if they were captured, and, indeed, many of them gave their lives for their country.

The Peace

The war ended in Europe on 8th May 1945. Europe was liberated from German occupation and Western Europe returned to democracy. Eastern Europe, having been "liberated" by communist Russia, had to wait another forty-five years for democracy. Germany, sitting in the middle, was divided into two - democratic West Germany and communist East Germany.

Britain did not win the war alone and could not have done so. The military might of the United States, in particular, was crucial to victory. However, in the summer of 1940, Britain stood alone in defence of European democracy and freedom. If Britain had surrendered or been occupied, it is by no means clear that Hitler would ever have been defeated. What *is* clear, is that history would have been very different.

Lightning Source UK Ltd.
Milton Keynes UK
UKOW02f0844280916

283989UK00001B/75/P